MEMORIES OF THE FUTURE

BY PAUL HORGAN

NOVELS

The Fault of Angels
No Quarter Given
Main Line West
A Lamp on the Plains
Far From Cibola

The Habit of Empire
The Common Heart
Give Me Possession
A Distant Trumpet
Memories of the Future

Mountain Standard Time (*a collected volume containing* MAIN LINE WEST, FAR FROM CIBOLA, *and* THE COMMON HEART)

OTHER FICTION

The Return of the Weed
Figures in a Landscape
The Devil in the Desert
One Red Rose For Christmas

The Saintmaker's Christmas Eve
Humble Powers
Toby and the Nighttime (*juvenile*)
Things As They Are

HISTORY AND BELLES-LETTRES

Men of Arms (*juvenile*)
From the Royal City
New Mexico's Own Chronicle (*with Maurice Garland Fulton*)
Great River: The Rio Grande in North American History
The Centuries of Santa Fe
Citizen of New Salem
Rome Eternal
Conquistadors in North American History
Peter Hurd: A Portrait Sketch from Life
Songs After Lincoln

MEMORIES OF THE FUTURE

by Paul Horgan

NEW YORK ❧ FARRAR, STRAUS AND GIROUX

Copyright © 1966 by Paul Horgan
Library of Congress catalog card number: 66–16295
All rights reserved

First printing, 1966

Published simultaneously in Canada
by Ambassador Books, Ltd., Toronto
Printed in the United States of America

TO
DORO

i

First to arrive were Wicklow and Diana Thayer, which was like them. They came down to Annapolis the afternoon before in their own car from Washington. Neither the Admiral nor Mrs Grace could be there to receive them, but Admiral Grace's aide, Commander Morton, did the honors satisfactorily.

"Adml Grace is delighted you could come," he explained, "and so is Mrs Grace."

From years of intimacy with the Graces, the Thayers knew this, but they smiled at the convention as it was uttered, and followed the aide up the burgundy red carpeting of the stairs to the second floor of the Superintendent's Quarters at the Naval Academy.

"Adml Grace is flying up from Norfolk in an hour or so," Commander Morton said. "He'll be here in time for dinner.

Mrs Grace is holding a committee meeting over in town with some faculty wives, at Commodore Bixby's house. She'll be back any minute, and wants you to have tea with her in the library. I know they both want to have a chance to talk to you, Adml Thayer, before Mrs Hopkinson gets here."

The Thayers exchanged a look.

"I should think so," said Mrs Thayer. "Poor darling."

"Thank you, Morton," said Admiral Thayer. "We'll want to be with her. It's why we came. I wish we were celebrating a different occasion. I do like to see this old house again. Do you remember, Diana?" he asked his wife, with one of his confidential airs that he frequently used with her in the presence of others, which never offended anyone, and made her conspiratorially happy with him. "When we used to come here, my first class year, to those horrible receptions? And Avy and Vivi would meet us here? There used to be palms in that corner," he explained to Commander Morton, pointing to the far end of the wide second floor hall, "and Admiral Grace, and his wife, and Doro, and Pete Millard, and Tom Richards, and those other fellows of our time, all brought the same girls, and we'd be scared to death coming in here, so we always managed to sit under, if not behind, the palms; choking to death, actually, in our stiff stocks. Diana, do you remember the time I spilled the ice cream? Mrs Eberle never forgave me. Or anyway she never forgot it. She mentioned it years later. I never knew why; it was my pants I spilled it on, not her precious red carpets. And now, by golly, we're here to stay a weekend. My first time back, too. Where are we sleeping?" he asked Diana, as though she, and not Commander Morton, would know.

"Let me show you, Adml," said Commander Morton, lead-

2

ing them up the next flight, with perhaps, thought Admiral Thayer, a little too much of a proprietary air. What were such fellows called in civilian life? Society men, that was it. But the wartime Reserve took in all kinds—had to. Admiral Thayer was determined to be agreeable.

The light came late and silvery through the window on the landing. It was a January Saturday in 1946. The mood outdoors was something like their feelings. The sky over the Severn was growing dark, there was winter sweetness in the light wind coming offshore, and a cold and ominous ripple played over the river and the bay. In one of the anchored vessels in the roads, a light before nightfall shone through a porthole. It suggested warmth, refuge from the cares outside, a world of snugness, where Commander Morton would rather be, at the moment, than here, where he was dreading the next twenty-four hours.

ii

Commander Morton had a horror of sentiment. Not that he was unsympathetic; rather, he considered that he was too much moved by other people's feelings, which he confessed always wore down his defenses. He had an easy way with all current jargons, including that of modern psychology, though he said this last made him nervous.

Phillips Morton had enjoyed discovering that old house at Annapolis. He'd come only recently as the Superintendent's aide, and as he was a reserve officer, he had never seen the quarters before. For that matter, he never expected to see the Academy, even when Admiral Grace had informed him in Okinawa that they'd be returning to the States to take up this new assignment at Annapolis, following the Japanese surrender. Morton, with a chaffing kind of delicacy, had reminded Vice-Admiral Grace that there'd be a lot of clatter and annoyance about bringing a non-Academy man back as aide.

"I'm not a wearer of the ring," he had stated with an edge of defiant guilt.

He'd told the Admiral that it would look pretty funny to a lot of people.

The Admiral had answered him, jiggling slightly in his high backed and bolted swivel chair on board ship, stating that he had every expectation of shocking some of his esteemed classmates. He considered, however, (with an accent of comedy in his grainy voice), that it would do more good to their livers than they would ever know. In any case, the Admiral concluded, he had already arranged for Morton to proceed to the Naval Academy. Morton always knew when the Admiral—the Adml—had closed an issue, and he had therefore murmured "Aye, aye, sir," with gratification at such topside loyalty.

Morton was both fond and afraid of him.

The Admiral was not very tall, but he always seemed quite tall enough, for his height was within himself. A handsome man in a weathered way, he had white hair, a dark pink face, deep blue eyes and very white teeth. His good friend Admiral Thayer once said that Avy Grace's smile was like the American flag—red, white and blue.

Morton was proud that the Admiral's portrait would some day join the others in this house. He enjoyed the varnished blue

4

and gold of the portraits, the sideburns, the ivory hilts of dress swords, heavily cascading gold epaulettes, clear simple gazes, and occasional glimpses of painted sea, cloud, and battle smoke; and he believed that nobody could for long be the familiar of these things without knowing a higher spirit and pride in the Navy—a sentiment he would never risk exposing to the kind of civilian world he came from.

He felt much the same about the rest of the house, too. As an official residence, it was full of objects which were constant among its furnishings, no matter who came and went as Superintendent of the Naval Academy. Morton liked to read the engraved silver plates on the glass cases containing ship models which lined the lower hall. In the big dining room, a massive silver service given long ago by a graduating class stood on the sideboard. In a corner of the formal drawing room was a painted French cabinet desk from another class. Most of the objects in the house made reference to men and women long gone but alive in the chronicle of the service.

If all this seemed to produce an atmosphere of state, Commander Morton—an expert on hostesses—marvelled the more at the skill with which Mrs Grace contrived to give the house a feeling of intimacy. She made the most of the large sun porch that opened off the formal drawing room. She put her own Brazilian furniture into the lesser, or informal, drawing room, with the chairs arranged so conversationally that they seemed to be interrupted if anyone came in. There were always bushes of flowers in the wide halls. In the daytime the generous windows were unshaded, and the sunshine came pouring in upon the red carpeting of the stair and the second floor.

In the small white panelled corner library, there were pleas-

5

ant little marks of domestic administration—letters on the desk, new books with page markers well advanced, a low table for cigarettes, tea, drinks or magazines, a telephone and some silver framed, signed photographs of personages and friends. These included the late President of the United States; the King of England in naval uniform; the Chief of Naval Operations; a handful of classmates, all admirals, including Wick Thayer; and Admiral Grace himself, on the bridge of his flagship carrier in the South Pacific. This all suggested that the members and possessions of a vice-admiral's establishment were transient on a grand scale. Nevertheless, Mrs Grace governed the house in her own image—formal but generous, orderly but considerate, and, finally, charming.

That there now existed, under these constant qualities, a concern which made her heart ache, the aide knew very well. Rather to his amazement, he discovered in the naval service that what moved him most was courage. He expected he was going to see much of it here in this quiet house.

iii

Mrs Grace reached home from her committee meeting shortly after five, and found Morton waiting for her.

"The Thayers are here," he reported.

"How pleasant. Will you send word that we'll have tea in ten minutes?"

"I've already told them you expected them. —The office

phoned. The Adml will be in around six. He's coming in the seaplane."

"Thank you, Phil. —The Committee was dreary. I mustn't have a headache, with my sister coming tomorrow. —Will you join us for tea?"

"I'd love to, Mrs Grace. Thank you."

She was moving about the rooms, touching flowers, the lights, the heavy satin curtains, a silver frame or two, a pile of books; and soon the angular ravages of the Filipino steward were undone by her touch, and the room became easy. At the window she parted the closed draperies.

"It's a cold evening. It's getting dark so early. —Poor darling Doro. I hope we can make everything seem warm, and light, when she comes. —I'll be down in a few minutes. Take care of the Thayers for me if they come down first."

She smiled upon him, and with an inclination of her head— a nod would never describe it—she left him.

She was perhaps a trifle taller than her husband. One of the famous Millard sisters of Washington, she was the blonde one. Her hair was not yet grey. Her eyes were a leonine blue. Her sister, Mrs Hopkinson, was as brunette as Mrs Grace was blonde. Commander Morton had never met Dorothy Hopkinson; but moving in the circles of flag rank all over the world, he'd heard so much about her that he felt that he knew her. Her husband had belonged to this generation of admirals, and had he lived, undoubtedly would have reached that rank himself. The Navy never let go of anyone who really belonged to it as Dorothy Hopkinson did, by virtue of her marriage, and her sister's, and the history of her own son.

Commander Morton was sensitive to airs and conventions.

7

He believed that he'd never known a group of people anywhere who maintained so casual and so consistent an intimacy as this particular part of the Navy world into which his assignment had thrust him. It was a world of nicknames; a vast network—like an organizational chart or a genealogical tree—with a diminutive at each little nerve-end that stood for an individual. Sometimes he thought it symptomatic of an eternal immaturity. Again, he considered that the friendliness and confidence which all those Spikes and Wicks and Docs and Tootsies and Evvies and Avys and Doros and J.J.'s stood for were values much more solid than a more formal convention usually implied. Perhaps he was being too sophisticated about it. If three-star admirals and their coevals chose to sound like schoolboys when they referred to each other, he might consider that after all, they were once all schoolboys together; which probably accounted for the whole thing. The fact was, when either the Adml or Mrs Grace called him Phil, he had to admit that he felt a small but lively pleasure.

iv

The Thayers appeared for tea ahead of their hostess.

"In here, Mrs Thayer," said Morton, showing them into the library.

It was amusing how everybody took everything up with Diana Thayer. She had a general smile, made of very dark, small eyes, a strong jaw and a big mouth, with fascinatingly irregular teeth. She powdered her face white and used a peony

8

red lipstick. Her hair was dark with a little grey. She had a handsome, neat little figure. Her hands were strong, very capable looking, and good sense and generosity seemed to animate them. There was never any doubt as to what she thought. Morton was glad to see her here. Her husband, too, for that matter, thought Morton, feeling generous.

The Thayers hadn't been to visit the Graces for so long that they had a few of the framed photographs to catch up on. The last one they picked up and looked at together showed a young officer, bareheaded, smiling, with something of the look about him of a blond lion cub.

"It is Davie," said Diana.

"He's exactly like a blond Doro, isn't he?" said Admiral Thayer, tilting his head and squinting a little to get a general blur which would enhance the likeness he found. "Don't you think so, Diny? —Commander?"

"I don't know, sir, I never saw Lieutenant Hopkinson or his mother, either, for that matter. I sort of think he looks sort of like Mrs Grace, though, a little."

Diana Thayer smiled with bitter sweetness.

"Wick, do you remember? He was the most adorable *little* boy I think I ever saw," she said. "Where's Vivi?"

"She'll be right down."

"Here I am, Diana," called Mrs Grace, coming in, leaning a little forward, with her cheek ready for the kiss each of the Thayers gave her. "—and Wick. I'm a little late," she stated with a clear and musical firmness. It was her humor to describe situations which were obvious. "Phil, will you ring for tea, please? —Avy will be here for dinner. Well. It isn't too late, my dear Wicklow Thayer," she added, smiling with fondness

9

at this old friend, "to congratulate you in person on your perfectly magnificent record in the Pacific. Diana has kept us informed, and of course I heard twice a week from Avy. It is so good to have you back. It will be so good to have everybody back, to stay, who is able to come home at all."

Dignity and melancholy sounded in her voice. Of them all, Wick thought, she had matured to her position better than any.

"Before you came," said Wick, "we were laughing about those other times in this house, when we were all such youngsters. How scared we were. And yet how—"

"—How we trifled," finished Diana, catching his eye and his thought.

"I think every woman has her plans all made for whatever might happen, at any time," said Mrs Grace, "don't you? When I came here with Avy as a girl, to those overwhelming parties, I knew exactly how everything in this house *ought* to be, and how I'd do it, if I ever got the chance."

"Are you? —Doing it, I mean," asked Admiral Thayer, grinning. Morton could not help grinning with him, for the way he opened his mouth and showed his tongue comically, like a toy dog with a red flannel lapper.

"Pretty much. Here is the tea. I'm not giving you a drink until Avy arrives."

She began to pour tea. Morton and the Filipino steward handed cups and sandwiches around.

"Well, my poor darling sister knows the mere fact," said Mrs Grace. "I suppose there isn't a ghost of a chance that it could be another false report?"

"No," replied Admiral Thayer. "This time it is really confirmed. Young Richards is back, too, you know."

"Of course. His father told me he has gone to see Eliza, with all the information he can give her."

"What those two women have been through," said Mrs Thayer.

"I think it very kind and wonderful of you both to come," said Guinevere Grace. "I know how much it will mean to Dorothy to have you here. I mean just simply to have you here, even if you said nothing to her."

"Well, we go back a long way together," said Admiral Thayer. "Not only Doro and Diny and I, but you and Avy, and all the rest of us. I'd have gone to see Doro at Coronado on the way East, if I'd have been able to, but my orders brought me right here. We only landed to fuel up in San Francisco. Diana and I came right on down from Washington the minute we—"

He finished it with a nod.

Mrs Grace turned to Commander Morton.

"I don't believe you've met my sister, have you Phil?"

"No, Mrs Grace. The only time I might have, was last June, when the Adml brought me back to the States with him on that flying trip. But when he stopped off to see her, he sent me on ahead to get things started here. But I have met lots of people around the world who adore her."

"They should. —It was the same when we were girls," said Mrs Grace. "We grew up in Washington, where Papá was a counselor in the State Department. My brother—he was older than we were—was appointed to the Naval Academy by President Taft. We used to come down to Annapolis for the hops."

"I'll never forget when I met you and Doro for the first time," said Diana Thayer. "It was over an Easter weekend, when we were all stopping with the Bixbys. We all thought Avy was madly in love with Phyllis Bixby."

"He was," said Mrs Grace. "He was until I told him he wasn't. He wouldn't speak to me for two months after that. Then the first thing he said was to ask me to wait for him." She smiled. "It had seemed to me possible that this might happen, so my plans were all made. Of course, I had told no one what I might have expected, not even Dorothy, but then we were always so different."

V

The sister of whom Mrs Grace spoke was three years younger. Dorothy as a girl was slim, like her sister Guinevere, but she had eyes so dark that they seemed to crackle with light. Her hair was nearly black, she wore it dressed low on her neck, and she bent her head habitually and smiled a little sideways, with a combination of shyness and shortsightedness. Young men used to say that she had a devastating myopia. The most striking thing about her, even then, was the way she considered first the desires and the feelings of others. Her sister had so much self-confidence that Dorothy more or less naturally assumed the role of handmaiden.

Doro, as everyone called her from childhood, imagined that all the midshipmen, or the handsome young men from the Government, or the younger New York newspapermen stationed in Washington, came to see Vivi rather than herself. Even after Vivi had promised to wait for Avery Grace and was thus bespoken in a more formal age which took its commitments seriously, Doro was sure nobody really wanted to come and bring her roses, or send her bonbons, or ask her to the theatre to see Sarah Bernhardt do *L'Aiglon* for the last time. All such things, which she coveted and enjoyed, she considered the proper due of her magnificent sister. Her young friends used to take her and shake her literally, and say to her that she was too self-effacing. Let her think of herself for a little while. A dash of selfishness, they said, would do wonders for her. But she smiled at them, and they were baffled by her, thinking she was too pretty, too healthy, too full of warmth and grace, to remain content in her diffidence.

The sisters went everywhere together. While waiting for Avery Grace, which meant the rest of his First Class year, and two years of service after that, Vivi Millard, with her almost royal sense of formality, accepted as escorts in Washington only older men, including a minor Italian prince who offered to take her back to Rome where he had an historic and crumbling palace, from which she could expect to be launched as an ambassadress if he might have the inestimable blessing of her assistance in his career. . . . But she preferred to wait for Avy, who paid her the honor of his period, and was gallantly jealous of the Roman. As for Dorothy, she saw no one particularly, but went to dinners, cotillions, at homes, up and down Massachusetts Avenue, around Dupont Circle, and to weekends at Annapolis with Vivi, being kind to the young gentleman of the occasion.

She was deeply in love with a midshipman who did not know her from any other prom girl. She welcomed the Annapolis excursions only in order to look at him, across the dance floor, or from the sidelines at regimental parade when he led his company for the pass in review. She had met him only once, at a tea one Sunday afternoon at the Superintendent's Quarters, had handed him a silver dish of chocolate *petit fours,* and had heard him introduced to another girl to whom he at once turned with a sweep of light across his glossy dark head. His smiling face was like a satyresque marble in a museum; an arrested likeness of youth, humor, appetite and power that committed Doro then and forever.

vi

His name was David Warren Hopkinson. He was to graduate with Avy Grace, Wick Thayer, Peter Millard, and the others of their crowd. She wondered if he had asked anybody to wait for him; but she felt sure he hadn't. Entirely unexperienced in amorous intrigue, as it was then racily called, she had nevertheless an instinctive understanding of the subtleties, and even the transgressions of love. She could read in her own passionately concealed attentions to David Hopkinson that he would never commit himself to any woman so soon, so young. His face was moulded in a sensual pattern. She believed that life was calling to him from so many different directions that he would have to answer each before he could make up his mind to settle down.

He was a famous Academy athlete. Avy Grace, Wick Thayer, everyone knew him very well; but he was busy with a girl in New York, and another in Baltimore. His friends at the Academy were all on the varsity football squad. Avy and Wick "went out" for boxing and wrestling, and though they were friendly, neither was especially intimate, with him. He had a reputation as the Don Juan among his classmates. Perhaps they resented him a little because, with all his attention to athletics, and all his femme-killing up and down the Atlantic Seaboard, he was academically distinguished. It seemed almost without effort that he mastered the complicated technical curriculum of the midshipman. He was naturally expressive, and in his English and history course, which represented the severely restricted culture of the Academy, he made a plausible case for himself as a cultivated young man. At suppers and upon other formal occasions when it was appropriate to do so, he would rise and make a speech, proposing the toast of the evening. Even though it was a commonplace of the naval service that all officers must be able and willing to do this on any occasion, Hoppy was the admiration of his fellows for his fluency, taste and charm on his feet. As a consequence of all such spectacular accomplishment, he was properly envied by his contemporaries.

A knowing circle of smiles would pass around the company whenever anyone mentioned him.

Avy and Wick would exchange a look.

Vivi and Doro would see them do it. Vivi would ignore it, already allowing the male world its tribal formalities and private references. But Doro would protest.

"Why do you all resent Hoppy so? You are simply envious of him. He is too clever."

"That's just it. He *is* clever."

"What's wrong with being clever?"

"Nothing."

"Then why don't you try yourself?"

"Oh, we don't have to."

This implied that there were better things to be. With an ache in her heart for him, Doro saw herself protecting him from the misunderstanding and jealousy of his fellow man, and her heart grew big on such noble sustenance; until she would remember that he had merely glanced at her once or twice, smiling his way on to someone else.

But her loyalty persisted, unrealistic as it might have been, born of a trifling moment, and nourished by what she imagined rather than what she knew; and it gave her an absent quality which, while it contributed to her unworldly charm, discouraged suitors after a time or two. Vivi thought to break through it—for Vivi noticed everything and had a plan for it—by arranging for a succession of beaux, trusting to God, nature and society that one of them would turn into something more significant. She even asked Doro if there was "anyone" of whom the rest of them knew nothing. Doro flushed a little, and warned herself that she would have to be more careful, if they suspected. Her pride arose, for she knew how they would tease her if she ever mentioned David Hopkinson to them; and she told her sister that there was nobody at all.

vii

The sisters went through June Week together, and seemed equally popular. But in Vivi's popularity there was the added interest of her now well-known agreement to wait for Avy, for the engagement was to be announced by Mr Millard at a reception in Washington the day following graduation. Avy was near the top of his class. He was one of the handful of

16

whom everyone felt, without any doubt at all, that they would really become admirals, so fulfilling in fact what the whole Academy always said of all midshipmen in fun.

It was a memorable week. The grounds were lustrous with the freshly-leaved trees. Lights hung in the branches and shone at night. That year the full moon was in the sky during June Week. The Severn was a frontier of romance and also of solemn duty.

At the Graduation Ball, Dorothy saw Hopkinson several times. He bowed and waved to her once, and half indicated his dance card as if to say that if it weren't entirely filled up, he would besiege her for a dance. The innocent conceit of the gesture, the assumption that she would have a dance waiting for him, made her heart contract with shame, for she knew that it was true; she would skip anyone's name to substitute his. But she danced with her brother Pete and Avy and Wick and their close friends, and they all said, Vivi included, that she had never looked prettier, or had been more popular. They all noticed that Tommy Richards had cut in on her several times. Perhaps "something" was beginning "there," on this momentous night. He was old Captain Richards' youngest son, and in addition to being a naval officer, he would some day be rich. They made their patterns early, innocently, in that society, for they all believed in the same things, to almost precisely the same degree. This was true not only of official life; but of private life.

The next morning, when the commissions were given out at commencement exercises, parents, sweethearts, in the audience, all leaned forward as their own midshipmen went up the ramp to shake hands with the Secretary of the Navy, salute, receive the parchment, and march down again officially confirmed.

The Superintendent read the full names . . .

". . . Midshipman Austen Avery Grace . . ."

Avy, beaming soberly, if that was possible, faced up to it, his chest lifted, seeming taller than he actually was. Vivi watching him nodded approval, proprietary and loving.

". . . Midshipman David Warren Hopkinson . . ."

If Vivi had looked at Doro, she might have known then. Doro was white and intense, smiling in a trance.

There he went, forever, most likely.

He was tall and slender. A sardonic modesty and charm played over his face. The applause for him was tremendous. He bent his head under it as he marched down the other side of the ramp, and glanced down at his commission as if entirely preoccupied, and mockingly surprised, by it. He was quickly lost among all the other white-uniformed graduates.

They watched next for Wick. Diana was sitting with the sisters. She was tacitly given to him, though nobody had ever said anything about it. Presently his name rolled out.

". . . Midshipman Wicklow Benson Thayer . . ."

Square, ruddy, almost humorously cordial, he shook hands with the Secretary, and to the delight of the crowd, was detained for an extra word or two, while the Secretary asked him how come he had gone this way, instead of into politics, like his granddaddy from Mississippi. Wasn't he, too, from Natchez? Yes, sir, he was. He added that perhaps he had chosen this way because it seemed so much less dangerous a life than making speeches in Mississippi. Genial, Secretarial laughter; another handshake; and Wick passed down the ramp to built-up applause with a story to tell them all later at lunch, at which they were going to have speeches and champagne.

In a tapering-off of high feelings, a little ruefully, the auspicious week was over. Families packed up and departed. The graduates went on their leaves before reporting for duty to their new assignments.

The Millard sisters went back to town, where Vivi's engagement party was held the next afternoon at the Chevy Chase Club. Half the First Class had been invited, for Avy had the world for his friends. Hoppy Hopkinson was expected, but instead of showing up he sent a telegram, stating that urgent family business had summoned him to Boston, and he deeply regretted. Avy handed the wire to Vivi, who handed it absently to Dorothy, who read it, and kept it the rest of her days. When they talked it over later, among other trifles of the occasion, they couldn't imagine what Boston had to do with Hoppy; nobody had ever known he had a family in Boston. Did it really say Boston? Yes, they would swear it did, though Baltimore was much more likely. Private smiles at this. The only way to settle it was to read the telegram again. Where was it? How odd. It had disappeared. But both Vivi and Doro were certain it had said Boston. Vivi said she was never apt to make a mistake like not remembering what a telegram said.

viii

How prophetic that perfunctory telegram seemed later on, Vivi thought, for it was in Boston two years later, or a little more, when she and Avy had been married, and were stationed there in the Navy Yard after his long cruise, and while Doro was visiting them, and sharing the excitement of their getting settled with the first of their own possessions, that Dorothy and David Hopkinson came together again.

Hopkinson was also stationed in Boston, on the staff of the Commandant of the Naval District. He was now two years older, though he actually looked older than that. He matured rapidly, in physical ways. He was as sensitive as ever to social climates and private emanations of attitude. He had already made the rounds of the eligible Boston girls. He hated to admit it, but among those whom he had met, there did not seem to be one whom he could fix in his mind's eye as this year's suitable date for Ensign David W. Hopkinson. Those who were really pure Boston he could not abide for their social pedantries, their serene and deadening implication of superiority. Those who were more interesting were also less acceptable socially. Farther down the scale, he could, and did, find companions who gave him what he wanted without much bother or expense; but these he could hardly take into society with him, however much he liked them and thought them worthy of his sincere if limited gratitude for pleasure delivered.

So it was that when Avy and Vivi arrived, he was pleased to see them again. Two years of distant, separate cruising had given a flattering perspective to their days of youth. They were sure that at the Academy they'd been the most intimate of friends. It was weeks before they exhausted the resources of their common experience, the roll call of names on which to linger through hours of talk and drink. When at last that was all caught up with, Dorothy arrived to stay for a long visit. Her heart beat when she heard that Hoppy was in town, and that her sister and her brother-in-law saw much more of him than of anybody else in Boston.

They all went to the Ritz-Carlton for dinner to celebrate her arrival. The shock—it was actually a shock—of seeing Hoppy, and of being with him, dining, drinking and dancing with him, after so long a time of daily giving him up, was almost more than Doro could bear. She was taciturn. She looked pale. She gave him confused glances and answered his talk in breathless banalities. The true meaning of this was lost upon Vivi and Avy, who wondered why on earth Doro was being so odd; but Hoppy's antennae were adjusted to every impulse of feeling between man—himself—and woman—any woman near him. He reconstructed those meager moments of that First Class year during which he'd seen this exquisite black and white girl as an accepted part of every large gathering. He recalled now that he had never seemed to notice her that she wasn't pouring at him the full riches of her lustrous dark regard. His pulse gave a thump at the thought that she might be in love with him. It seemed natural enough. Plenty of others had been. His manner sweetened in various gentle ways. He would put her at ease. It was the least he could do. He saw an almost miserable look of stricken gratitude in her eyes. Her whole goodness, her warmth, the selflessness which everyone else knew in her, smote him. She made him in that first difficult evening a greater gift than he had had from anyone else he'd ever known. He was not a humble man; but he was now brought low by qualities of virtue which always before had been subjects of humor to him; humor, or scorn. Now they stirred pity in him; not for her, but for her picture of him, which he was sure was ever so different from what he really was. At the same time, he rehearsed thoughtfully how piquant it would be to kiss, not so much beauty, but so much goodness. It was a temptation he had never before encountered.

He fell in love with her that night.

Dorothy's two months as the guest of the Graces were soon gone. The four of them went everywhere together, at first; but presently, Hoppy made occasions to take Doro out alone. They dined at the Copley-Plaza. They drove out to Framingham to an inn. She took him to concerts of the orchestra, where the august splendors of the music under Doctor Muck spoke her love for her, and afforded Hoppy an extension of his range of topics with a new vocabulary. As winter deepened they could go ice skating. They told each other they were very happy. They went to parties at the Commandant's and even met a few Bostonians, who while recognizing that these Navy people could never actually hope to belong there, still were moved to admit with a sort of irritable courtesy that it was no doubt pleasant for them to have this opportunity to know Boston even slightly. It was a delight to Doro and Hoppy to be able to gasp together at such local manners. They loved Boston not only for its own charms, but for the fact that there they had come together.

They announced their engagement to Vivi and Avy. Vivi declared that though they—she could speak for Avy too—they were simply delighted to hear this, none of them could acknowledge it until it had been approved by Papá in Washington. Hoppy looked at Doro to see if this were a fact. It was. They made plans for him to go down to Washington if he could get three days' leave, and call upon Mr Millard with his news and his request. The wedding would take place in Washington, whenever it might be.

They were married the following April, and went to Bermuda on their honeymoon. They returned to duty in Boston, and were transferred to the Mare Island Navy Yard at San Francisco in the following autumn. They had a little under two years there. Hoppy was ordered to duty in the destroyers a couple of months after war was declared in 1917.

Doro stayed behind in San Francisco to close their apartment. Because Hoppy at first was assigned to convoy duty, and was ashore in the United States every few weeks, she returned to the East Coast to stay with Vivi in Newport, where Avy was on the staff of the War College, and chafing to go to sea. He was actually making prophetic studies in naval aviation which helped to prepare him and the Navy for operations in another ocean and a later war. The sisters plunged into war duties.

When Hoppy came ashore, they all met for parties in New York, and though the Graces would have to return to Newport after a day or two, Doro stayed on as long as her husband was there for her to see. They were so deeply in love that the strain of being separated told on them more than the work they were doing for the war. He would sometimes confess to her that he could not recognize himself these days. If he had been able to stand off, five years ago, and look ahead to what he was now, he would never have believed it possible. He had no essential secrets from her, as to his nature; though as a considerate husband there might have been details and episodes which he withheld from her; and so he could quite freely admit to her that he was by inclination something of a libertine and a sensualist, as well as a pretty vain if not conceited fellow, and to see him now, so in love with one woman, desiring to be what she expected him to be, and all that, he could only declare was amazing.

Such admissions went deep to her heart, until it felt constricted, and she could hardly get her breath for a moment.

She would say to herself that she must never expect more of anyone, a man, her husband, especially, than he could naturally give. Perhaps some day there might be a limit to it. Perhaps it would gradually become less than what he gave her now. If it should ever so befall them, then she must remember how it was now, and try to realize that love was not to be measured in quantities; but in qualities.

Every time she had to let him go, as he returned to duty at sea, she knew that he might be drowned in the submarine warfare of that North Atlantic campaign.

Every time he came back it was like meeting all over again.

Finally, he brought news that his next sailing would take him away for a long time. He had an assignment about which he could say nothing, except that he would be away for a good while; here was an end to these frequent reunions. Grinning like a satyr, loving her with every reference of his style and criterion of comfort, luxury, taste and excitement, he declared that they'd better make this a good one. By this he meant, principally, to spend more money than they could afford, buying things for each other, living in a suite at the St. Regis, and having champagne and scotch and many friends to drink it with them; going to the theatre and the opera; and if the nights were brief, after they got back to the hotel, the mornings were long. Winter was outside in the air above Fifth Avenue, and whether sunny or cold, or dark, snowy and wet, that was a matter of indifference to them; here they were together, each the other's habit, creating much to remember.

When he sailed, she was not permitted to see him to his ship. He was to report soon after midnight on a certain date. They had the evening alone. He was an exact and brilliant officer. He always allowed himself an extra fifteen minutes over his generous margin of safety in time to join his ship.

That night he followed his custom.

He kissed her goodbye in their small, darkened, silk sitting room in the hotel, and said it would be much easier for him if she didn't even come to the elevator with him. She shut the door behind him, and stood in the darkness, praying for him, whatever he was going to on the sea. She heard the brass elevator gates clang (like the ones in Paris she recalled from a trip with Mamá years before) and in her thoughts said goodbye to him again.

The sound really said he was gone, and she began to weep, as she had never done in his presence.

At that moment, the door opened, the light from the hall cut past him, and he shut it out quickly. With a laughing sort of desperation he took her in his arms. He whispered to her in the dark that when the elevator came he could not take it; he had motioned it on. He had come back to use his fifteen minutes here. Her tears heightened his love into passion all over again. He did not even throw off his heavy blue and gold overcoat. The lights were out. A glow from the sky above the electric streets outlined the window, and made a silhouette of the rose tree he had sent her which stood on a low table across the room. They knew love again on his borrowed quarter of an hour, but with few words, and to great avail, before he left her at last.

X

"David was a large baby, and perfectly blond," said Vivi, nodding toward the photograph on the table across the room. Commander Morton gave it a glance. He saw that smiling, healthy, beautiful face, like a mask of comedy, abstract and timeless, a family household god. "We were all so amused that the baby was so blond, when both Hoppy and Doro were utter brunettes. Everyone made the usual jokes, and everyone turned to me, because I am so blond, to determine that everything was quite all right. If you understand what I mean."

There was a remote sound below, in the house.

They all glanced toward the door of the small library which gave on to the hall. It was dusky both inside and outside by now. The red carpets of the hall shone in the lamplight.

"It must be the Adml, returning," said Morton.

"It is surely Avy," said Mrs Grace. "I had begun to worry, though of course for no reason."

Diana smiled at her, wife to wife, for their husbands both spent much time in aircraft, and every time, until they were known to be on earth again, their women lived with a sixth sense alert for something best kept undefined.

Admiral Grace came rapidly up the stairs, across the dark glowing hall, and into the white-panelled sitting room. They

26

all, except his wife, rose. He affected not to notice this, as this was a personal, not an official, occasion and he must not collect tributes. Still, something about him, as well as his position, impelled even the Thayers, his oldest friends, to stand a little ceremoniously. He greeted them affectionately, kissing Diana, and pumping Wick's hands. He nodded cheerfully to his aide, and then bent down to kiss his wife, finally sitting beside her on the white linen sofa.

"I see you have all been drinking a cup of tea," he declared as if he were a seriously observant man.

"Vivi wouldn't give us a drink until you got home," said Admiral Thayer. "Thank God you made it."

"We've time for one before dinner," said Vivi. "I've been talking them to death. —Phil, would you ring for the tray?"

"When does Liza arrive?" asked Admiral Grace.

"Later this evening, quite late, I believe," answered Vivi. "She is driving down from Wilmington with young Duncan Richards."

"Of course, that is the best thing about it, if anything is, isn't it?" said Diana, leaning forward. "I mean, that Doro has Liza. They are so wonderful together, I don't think either of them'll ever be so awfully lonesome as they would be if they didn't have each other."

Commander Morton understood that Liza had been married to young David.

"She's a marvellous girl," said Admiral Grace. "Both my boys are in love with her, to one degree or another."

Diana smiled at Vivi.

"Is there anything *there?*" she asked with her dark eyebrows lifted.

"My dear," said Vivi, in her coolest, most musical tone, "I

27

can't think of anything less likely to appeal to any of us, just now."

"How was your trip, Avy?" asked Wick.

"Very agreeable."

Admiral Grace had an air of modest but complete satisfaction. This was habitual. Arrangements contrived, as if by themselves, to suit him, wherever he went. How much complicated effort by how many people it took to see that things were agreeable for him, he did not apparently know; or at least acknowledge. It seemed to him better manners to take for granted everything due to him as a vice-admiral than to make a fuss and embarrass everybody every time the ancient protocols were observed. That was how things were; let the natural history of flag rank carry the day.

The result was that Avery Grace had developed a sense of confidence which fitted him like a splendidly made coat. His high tanned color, his amused blue eyes, his white hair, cut rather short and brushed up, his mouth which was set with upward corners, his speech, full of unemphatic strength, all contributed to this effect, which was that of a classic conception of naval rank in its highest forms.

The boy came in with the cocktail tray. The Admiral gave him a friendly nod, and watched the tray to its secure deposit on the low table in front of the couch.

"I flew down before lunch to Norfolk with Tommy Richards—"

(the same Tommy Richards, now a rear-admiral, who had once paid Dorothy his cubbish attentions)

"—to look at the new carrier before she is launched. We were received by Charlie Featherington, went over the whole

28

ship with him, lunched at the club, did some dictating, played nine holes of golf with Charlie, had a shower and a drink, and flew back with no trouble at all. Though I think I prefer my own plane. These seaplanes are nicely made, of course, but they are so slow. You're always leaning forward to make them go a little faster."

"Really, Avy, at your age," murmured his wife, who was now busy with the tray of ice and glasses and things to drink.

"Age? I'm no age, especially. Do you think I am, Diana?"

He turned to her and then looked at Commander Morton to take him in on his side of the joke.

"What did *you* do all day, Phil, without me here?" he asked.

Vivi answered for the aide, giving him glasses to hand around.

"He's been inordinately helpful to me, planning for to-morrow. —We were just talking about David. Do you remember, Avy, how dumfounded everyone was when little Davie was born so blond?"

The Admiral chuckled.

"I never heard so much cackling over anything in my life. Here you are still cackling. —I got home from France just in time for the christening, which even at that was a little late. Davie must have been almost a year and a half old before we sprinkled him. And got sprinkled generously in return, I might add. —I was the godfather," he added, for Morton's benefit. "I naturally had to hold him for a moment. He didn't yell, he watched the Bishop (we had bishops at our beck and call, in those days)—"

"Friend of my family's," inserted Vivi, preserving a proper respect for bishops.

"—with sort of a critical air, do you remember, Diana? You are my god-wife. He was a big baby. We pledged him in champagne to a career in the Navy. Diana gave him a table-spoonful and he lapped up every drop of it. I'll never forget some of the speeches we made that day. I never heard Hoppy funnier or more wonderful. I always think it was one of the finest beginnings I'd ever known. You know how sometimes things take a particular shape for you."

They knew what he meant. Wick said to himself that that was Avy's gift, which had made him so useful and so success-ful professionally, he could make things take a particular shape, and so mean something to others; he'd done it time and again in peacetime training for naval air operations; he'd done it out there in the last couple of years, where the enemy supplied the meanings and the ends.

"Well, you certainly took your godfathering seriously," said Wick.

"I followed him like one of my own two boys. You'll meet my own sons, Phil, when they come ashore in due course. I'm sorry you won't ever meet young David now. He really grew up into one of the finest youngsters you can imagine. We've always been very close, both families. I could write a book about all our doings. It looked at first as if Hoppy wouldn't get home from the other side in time to let us hold the christening on the date decided upon. He was in hospital in Paris for a couple of months. That duty of his in the North Sea really did him in. I saw him there, and I was really quite worried."

There had been months of patrolling in the winter weather of the North Sea, and even through the last summer, the weather was turbulent and cold. Destroyer duty was especially arduous. Hoppy was on the bridge for days at a time. He lived on coffee, cigarettes, and technical interest in duty. The intensity which had fascinated Dorothy he gave equally and perhaps even more to his profession. Every problem at sea was to be met not only squarely or adequately, but superbly. Just as it had always been more than enough that he gave to games, or to women, so must he do the same in his command afloat. He was drenched through by the icy sea water day after day. He would not take enough time for proper meals. He drove his men. Many of them grumbled about it, but they all respected him because they were aware that he demanded even more of himself than of them.

When the Armistice came, he was exhausted. Spending leave in Paris, he should have gone to bed to sleep, read, eat, for days. But instead, he set out to do the town, since that was what one always did in Paris. It was what he had promised himself during those cold, hazardous nights at sea.

He was too ill to celebrate for long.

Avery Grace found him in the military hospital at Neuilly and thought he was going to die, from the way he looked. He had developed an acute case of arthritis that kept him twisting slowly, repeatedly, to find a position, a relation of bone to bone, that might hold the promise of some day being, for a moment, only a second or two, a bit more comfortable.

He was given no more duty in Europe, but was sent home on sick leave as soon as he could travel. Avy had got home ahead of him. The plans for the christening were all made. Hoppy was impatient to see his son. There was, he knew, to be the damnedest party ever given. Everybody was in Washington. Christmas and New Year's were just over, and Peace was here again, and festivity stayed alive in the air and in everybody's mood. Doro could hardly wait to see him. But when they met, in the Union Station at Washington, she was subdued at his appearance. He seemed almost an old man. He was gaunt, his face was deeply lined, he was alternately stooped and exaggeratedly erect, his eyes had dark gouges of suffering under them. She had been prepared by Avy, but nobody could ever adequately prepare those in love for what they would find in place of what they remembered or imagined. Hoppy saw in her face the first real opinion of how ill he had been. He bitterly remembered his former magnificence, in looks, vitality, charm. Unfairly, yet without responsibility, since he was ill, he resented Doro for her health, which was an affront to the way he felt now.

Why must things change? they asked themselves, and the Graces asked each other.

But perhaps things were not so different, or so disappointing after all, for after a few days of learning each other's language again, and of marvelling over the baby, his old spirits began to revive. His pain was going away for an hour or two at a time. The doctors were encouraged. They cautioned him about taking anything to drink at the christening, but that was nonsense; he had to have a glass of champagne at his son's christening. He had several, and then many more, and never in his life felt better. The speeches were really something, and his was the best one of all—they all told him so. It was like a return of complete happiness, though Doro and the Graces dreaded what might follow, when the gaiety was over, and the cost of it remained.

But there was nothing to fear right then. Hoppy seemed to suffer no ill effects. He was once again the most amusing, the most durable, the most handsome officer of his grade, which by now was lieutenant-commander. Perhaps he would have been a full commander, like Avy, if he had not been off on that more or less obscure North Sea patrol duty. Anyhow, he was sure his time would come.

The Navy granted him more sick leave, and then as he improved, assignments in more or less tropical climates so that he would have every chance to recover.

One of his most pleasant was spent in Honolulu, where he and the baby and Doro, and the whole Grace family, happened to be stationed at the same time. The Graces by now had two sons, one David's age, and the other a baby. Little David and his cousins lived in swimming pants all day long. They played in the sun, and though they didn't know it, they were growing strong, beautiful and happily privileged in what amounted to a hereditary society. It had its cold small calculations, like any career order, and it had its attachments which were rudely torn apart by the transfer of officers and their families. But wherever it showed itself, it was a medium in which the officers and their wives were sustained in security and confidence. A little world of professional specialists, it had its own laws for its perpetuation. The sons of naval officers could do no better than to enter the service when the time came.

As his health, in spite of what seemed like periodic improvement, slowly declined, Hoppy devoted himself to making his son strong and single-minded about the future. There were those who felt sometimes that he was too harsh with the child. But young David was blessed with a golden temperament that seemed to echo the golden quality of his looks—yellow hair, tawny, tanned face and body, hazel eyes and an odd little smile, hovering proudly and even with a little secret meaning on his big friendly mouth, as if he were too proud to show anything but smiling acquiescence to his father and to anyone else who might direct his course.

Hoppy believed that it was possible to be as efficient in the training of a child as in the performance of any other technical task. He invented a regimen, with time-tables, charts, schedules, physical examinations, endurance tests, progress checkups, whereby he geared this boy to the future. Everyone was ready to admit that the system—or something—produced results; for

David grew sturdily and harmoniously. He seemed to look upon the plan as a game, at first, and entered into a sort of phantasy of competition with himself that exactly caught his father's spirit, which was competitive to an extraordinary degree. Another word for it would be aggressive, as any of his classmates would have said. Doro wondered at times just how much good all this spartan regimen would do, and whether she might not be acquiescing in what amounted to a usurpation of her own duties and rights as a mother. Davie's little-boyhood might have been more of a season of sweetness and pleasure to her, and perhaps to him too, than the regimen allowed. It was as if she had done her elementary duty in giving birth, projecting the child successfully through extreme infancy until the time of beginning physical independence; whereupon the tribal lord assumed privilege and responsibility, and moulded the young warrior in other ways than woman's.

There were a few quarrels over it. Doro's dark eyes could crackle and glow with fury; her voice would strike him at such times with astonishing force. But she had no weapon against Hoppy's infinite sarcasm, the polish, the perverse charm, of his insults, which he accompanied with a calculating smile that was infuriatingly self-confident; and with reason; for this was merely a more civilized way than the caveman's for a husband to beat a wife, and create that suffering on which passion would later feed in forgiveness, delight and renewal.

The family went from Hawaii to China where Hoppy was part of the naval mission. When they were ordered back to the United States after several years, there were reunions, parties, exclamations over how Davie had grown, and thanks for the exotic gifts which they brought back—miniature trees made of jade, crystal and semi-precious stones, carved to represent leaves, buds, flowers, and drops of dew; carved ivory; cigarette boxes made of silver and embellished with green and white jade; embroideries; dishes of rose quartz.

But the real purpose of the return was to have Hoppy's health thoroughly examined. He went to Bethesda for four weeks. The results were not altogether hopeful, though he was assured that he would not be retired immediately. The next assignment he was given took him to Mexico, as naval attaché. It was a post which suited them all. They liked the Ambassador, his daughters, and his wife. There was a sort of decorous gaiety about the whole mission in which Doro's charm was much exploited. Hoppy's gallantries set a mark for the American society in the Mexican capital.

He used to say, with a comic twinge of pain which his intimates knew was no joke, that he was actually sacrificing himself here for his country.

There was more than humor to this.

The parties, the amount of diplomatic drinking, the challenging ingenuities of Mexican diet, the exciting altitude of the city, together with his inevitable drive, his competitive nature, brought him to spend more strength than he had, and to aggravate his malady, and force its issue much sooner than almost any other life might have done.

David, close to his teens, began to see his mother rather gallantly, in between times of his exercises, his study, the unceasing labors which his father set for him.

Doro was grateful for this. She could not help the private realization that it might not be too long before her son would be all she had. She loved him with all her heart, but the truth was, she had two hearts, one for him and one for her husband. She would ask herself sometimes if she could ever imagine that one could take the place of the other, if death made it necessary. In vain she begged Hoppy to be more careful; to harbor his resources. He assured her that if she kept on worrying she would feel worse than he did, and what's more, would begin to show it, which would infuriate him. It was a part of his pride that she be as beautiful and smart as possible.

The parties kept on.

There were big dinners at the Embassy, which were most temperate. But these were followed by later gatherings of the younger set, mostly the military and naval crowd, which would go on until daylight. They would find a restaurant decorated with paper roses and glass grapes, lighted by oil lamps and candles, and panelled in strips of dark stained wood, and they would engage the whole place for the night, order music, a devastating menu, and every drink on the card, and give themselves over to singing, dancing, toasts, and endless anecdotes, recited for the benefit of the whole gathering by any member who felt moved to rise, glass in hand, and give voice.

Such occasions were frequently memorialized by a group photograph. The Mexican photographer was a favorite who brought hampers-full of equipment. His eyes watered pitiably when the flash powder went off, until everyone said that he was in the wrong profession. Still, he made each one lean forward so as to be surely in, and he was extravagant with the number of plates he expended in his anxiety to get a really fine picture. They always made him sit down after the picture-taking and join them in a glass of tequila.

Three days afterward, when the photographs were ready, he would deliver them to Hoppy, the natural leader of the society, to make selections for quantity printing. They were invariably more hilarious than flattering. The faces were chalk white, the backgrounds were dark, the expressions were like a collection made at a zoo.

Young David would often gaze upon the pictures and wonder how anybody could call that sort of thing having fun. It looked silly to him, and a little pathetic, even unseemly. He was entering into that time of life when much that was taken for granted by adults seemed a trifle insane to the young.

Such pictures were later to be among his most vivid reminders of his father; and in them he would find real reminders of that boisterous, generous, and suffering man.

For the suffering grew steadily worse all through the Mexican experience. When a presidential campaign resulted in a new incumbent back in Washington, it brought an official opportunity for the Ambassador to resign, and by the same token, for a reshuffling of the staff. The Hopkinsons were ordered home; Hoppy to the hospital again; and this time, the verdict was final and certain. He was retired immediately. He knew that nobody was deceived. He might have a few years; but he would never be much good again. He had one more job to do, and he was going to live to do it. After that, he would take what might come.

xiv

His great aim was to secure an appointment for David to the Naval Academy. Ironically, it was more difficult to get one for the son of an officer than for any other boy. He canvassed the situation in every small detail. They were in Washington for a few weeks staying with the Graces, and he took the opportunity to see various Members of Congress, who responded with various equivocations which when translated meant that politically there was not much advantage to the appointment of a Navy Junior when votes at home were considered.

He talked it over with Avy Grace, who was then a captain, assigned to the office of the Navy Department concerned with air plans. Avy wondered why it mightn't be a good idea to settle down out West somewhere, in one of those sparsely populated states, say, Arizona or New Mexico, and concentrate attention on the Congressional delegation from that state, beginning right now. Davie would be ready to enter in a couple of years. The Senators were safely in office for more than that length of time, and the Congressman was like to be reëlected for as long as he liked.

Hoppy was at once excited over this idea.

He remembered a summer he had spent on a ranch in New

39

Mexico with a roommate from his Eastern prep school. He imagined now that all his life he had subconsciously been wanting to return to the Southwest. He hadn't thought of the roommate for years, but now it seemed to him that there must be a design in all the events of his life, for, remembering that vast and brilliant land, the essential life of man and beast, where competition was reduced to its starkest terms, and a man was baron of his own domain, and the sky was so clear, and the light so warm, he had in his mind the hope that a new beginning could bring; for himself, his health; for his son; and for—for everything.

He wrote at once to the roommate of long ago, whose address he still kept in his blue morocco and gold address book, asking for advice as to where he could buy a few acres, a nice little house, in a clement region; and how he could make the incidental acquaintance of the Members of Congress from New Mexico in such a way that they would be inclined to take him and his purpose seriously.

The Graces would never forget how difficult he was to live with while waiting for a reply to his letter. Laughingly they all begged him to be patient. Ranchers often had other things to do but write letters.

He replied that that might be true, but Abbott wouldn't let him down. They had been inseparable in school. He would do anything on earth for Jack Abbott, and he was sure Jack Abbott would do as much for him—Jack, that short, stocky, serious, apple-faced boy who years ago had taught him to ride a horse, kill a rattlesnake, and play four chords on a guitar.

They all smiled because Hoppy was so obviously not allowing for any of the changes which might in the meantime have befallen Abbott.

It was Hoppy's turn to smile when the letter came. It was three pages long. It answered his requests clearly and hopefully, and invited him to come and bring his family to stay as long as they liked until he had had a chance to look around and make up his mind about what he was going to do. It also said that for arthritis, the climate was beneficial in many cases. An in-law of Abbott's had come out to stay years before, pretty badly crippled, but the sunlight, the dry air, the relaxation of life on the ranch had done wonders for him. Abbott also knew the senior Senator well, who lived in Santa Fe. Some time he and Hoppy could take a run up there in the car and call on the Senator in his own house and talk things over.

XV

Moves were familiar enough in the Army and Navy. One more meant little to Doro. She only wished she had the same stern optimism in her breast as Hoppy, when they set out for the Southwest late that summer. He felt her lack of it. It made him say bitter things, or keep a bitter silence.

They motored all the way.

Young David, with newly-discovered cynicism hidden beneath his golden passivity, kept a record of how many hundred miles they might drive at a time without any word spoken between his father and mother. He imagined what it would be like if they piled up in a car wreck, and how he would rescue them both, and by his inspired effectiveness in the emergency, reconcile them and thus win them back from death. Returning to the actual world, his thoughts would assess what he knew of love and family; and he formed the resolve which he later told them of.

He would never marry.

They asked him why.

He replied that he had seen enough of it right here, and did not feel he could honestly say that he thought it an attractive life, or one with much love in it.

His mother burst into tears. His father wanted to punish him physically for such unfeeling words. He had hurt them both bitterly.

They concealed from themselves none of the memories they both had of quarrels, disappointments and changes in feeling from time to time. But they considered that all such matters were of no importance measured against the profound habit each had for the other, and their own respect for the tradition of themselves together, which had begun so ardently in Boston so many years ago. They regarded themselves as ideally married, and looked at their son with astonishment that he should have judged them so dispassionately and so wrongly.

Their reaction to his famous declaration disturbed young David more than he could afford to show.

Actually, saying it and then suffering because of having said it, was the first episode of his own maturity. Who knew what crust of childish impropriety it broke through within him, so that other, worthier feelings could find freedom in his character? At all events, from that time on, not only on the remainder of the trip West, but during all their time that was left to them together as a family, he became the very son they longed for him to be, who blessed them with his good nature, tolerance, hard work and leaping intelligence.

xvi

Hoppy was a force in his world, wherever he might be.

Abbott, his old friend, introduced him to all the suitable people in the little city of Crystal Wells on the high plains of southeastern New Mexico where he made up his mind to stay. Soon enough, everyone he met was helping him to settle his problems. Abbott, though he lived most of the time on his ranch west of town in the mountains, owned much property in Crystal Wells. Hoppy found seven acres north of town, flat as a table top, with a small square white frame house on it enclosed by cottonwood trees. There was a pump with a windmill out in back, a vestigial chicken yard, an acequia that carried brown water from the creek a mile away, and everywhere freedom for the eye—east to the pink bluffs of the Las Vacas River, northward to the level violet horizon, westward to the blue lift of the mountains seventy miles away, and southward across the valley of the town with its green crowned trees. Abbott said he knew the man who owned this place. It was sold to the Hopkinsons on comfortable terms. If Hoppy suspected anything, he did not avow it. The deed to the property showed it as belonging to a corporation. But Dorothy was sure Abbott himself owned the place, and had practically given it to them. She was touched, perhaps a little ashamed. But Hoppy was full

43

of plans, content to accept matters. Whenever he was obsessed by an idea or a project, health itself seemed irrelevant. Together he and Dorothy once more plunged into the task of creating a new home out of the possessions which had come and gone with them all over the world.

xvii

In the next couple of years, the Hopkinsons' place, which they christened Little Farm, became an oasis for Navy people travelling between the East and West Coasts. The Graces came several times, the Thayers twice, Peter Millard drove through on one of his vacations from the Naval District headquarters at New Orleans. All of the various visitors felt at home the moment they arrived, however much they might have wondered what Doro and Hoppy could make for themselves here on these sunswept plains, so bare, so vast, so remote from everything the Navy had given them before.

Did not Hoppy miss the seacoast and a sense of the ocean?

Where was Doro's society, that system of rank and reciprocity which had expressed her world for so long?

Such questions were never spoken. Visitors found the house as attractive, formalities as pleasantly observed, a sense of mission and determination as evident here, as in any other atmosphere the Hopkinsons had ever lived in.

But they were privately shocked at Hoppy's condition. He made light of it, refused to talk about it, gave forth as much energy in local gallantries and duties as ever. He could not conceal, however, the unconscious and unremitting effort he made to get away from the pain that twisted him as if it were a steady wind and he an oceanside cypress.

Everyone's first impulse was to beg him to be more quiet. He should give fewer parties, stop drinking entirely, not work so hard all day in his garden under the sun that blackened him to a spuriously healthy color.

But they soon saw that these were his only prides and respites, and they let him be, while he peopled his house for parties, with everybody in long dresses and black ties, and using one after another of his famous dry martini cocktails, of which he drank quantities without either getting drunk, or becoming free from his inner rack.

xviii

In August of that last summer at Little Farm, Millard Grace, Avy's older son, and Duncan D. Richards, son of that classmate of Avy's, came to stay a month with young David. All three boys hoped to be appointed to the Naval Academy. (Avy's other boy, Thayer Grace, would try two years later.) A week or so after the young visitors arrived, Hoppy decided to take them to the northern part of the state to have a week's fishing. On the way back he would pause at Santa Fe to see the Senator about an Annapolis appointment for David, who was in his last year of high school, and would be ready the following June to enter the Academy.

Doro thought the trip would be hazardous for Hoppy to undertake. So did David. Their protests made no impression.

Hoppy organized the expedition with professional thoroughness. He made the boys pack and unpack everything half a dozen times because the better they packed the more room they would save in the car. Duncan D. Richards pointed out that there was room to spare even as it was, and that there was no real reason for him to do it all over again. He was told that the best reason to do it all over again was because he was told to do it. To a Navy Junior, this was understandable. They repacked. Doro saw them off, and then left by train to spend a week in Coronado with the Thayers, where Wick, a captain, was in command of one of the new cruisers based at San Diego.

No news came from the fishing expedition, and none was expected. They were high in the mountain meadows of northern New Mexico, out of touch with mail or telegraph. They hadn't been encamped for more than a day when the boys wished they could reach Doro to tell her that Hoppy ought to go home, or something. The rough mountain roads had exhausted him, for though the boys tried to insist that they be allowed to spell him at the wheel, he refused to let anybody else drive. He handled the wheel for mile after mile over the stony ruts of the back country. His pain was extreme.

When they encamped, he worried the boys by going into the ice cold mountain streams to fish. He stated that if that was what he had come for, it would be idiotic not to do it, then.

David made up his mind to have a quiet, serious talk with his father, drawing him away from his cousin Millard and young Richards. The effort amused Hoppy, and when he realized its purpose, enraged him. His black eyes turned red in

46

their depths, smoldering like coals in a banked fire. He scolded his son with sardonic fury, in a voice that sank from exhaustion into a strident whisper. David believed that none of it was to be taken personally. He saw the bitter vanity of his father's whole desire to drive himself as he had been able to do with safety years before. He resolved never again to risk such a scene, but to watch unceasingly, in case he might suddenly need to make a crucial decision.

Through the miserable remaining days of the fishing expedition, the three boys were uneasy at what was so plainly a piece of perverse foolishness. Hoppy himself seemed at times ready to quit and go home, but for the promise he had given them that they should have a week of the best trout fishing in the country.

It was true that they caught all they could want. They made plans for how they would wrap their last day's haul in wetted moss, and eventually in ice which they would buy from the first filling station they saw. When they reached Crystal Wells, they would be able to visit several houses in town, bringing fresh trout as gifts from those far-away mountain streams where no cares were—except those which man brought with him.

They drove at last into Santa Fe. Hoppy telephoned from a drugstore to see if the Senator was at home, and in accordance with his letter, if he could call to see him. After a pause, the secretary said that Commander Hopkinson might come right up for a little conference, though the Senator would be obliged to excuse himself after about half an hour, for another appointment with an Indian delegation from San Felipe.

The boys knew how ill Hoppy felt when he came out of the drugstore and told David to drive.

47

He also said that he wanted David to go into the house with him to see the Senator.

David had not expected this. He demurred.

In an air of final bafflement and defeat, his father shook his head, and let it hang forward as if to say that he might as well stop trying to do anything for anybody if this was how his efforts were to be rewarded. David quickly recovered himself, and said he really would like to go in after all; saying to himself that judging by his father's exhaustion, it might even be necessary to help him in and out of the Senator's house. At this, he blushed with shame; for he knew that was what his father, without saying so, was bringing himself to admit was necessary.

The other boys stayed out in the car. David took Hoppy's arm, as if casually, and walked with him slowly up to the deeply-arched portal of the house. Hoppy halted them to rest for a second.

He closed his eyes.

Then he bit his jaws, straightened up, and scowled with his old sardonic charm, and rang the bell. He was transformed from a stooped, skeletal invalid into a figure of confidence and power.

David always remembered how he had witnessed a supreme effort in his behalf.

The interview was brief. The Senator, a cultivated man, was a little remote. But the burning energy in Hoppy's eye made its impression on him. He was listening to a dying man. The boy was evidently promising in every way. He was certainly magnificent looking, and he answered a few perfunctory questions with a collected charm. There was already a Senatorial commitment to appoint a certain young man from Rio Arriba County; but it might work out that the First Alternate would have a chance at the appointment were the other young man to fail in the entrance tests. To the position of First Alternate, he would appoint young Mr. Hopkinson, and in the event of his succeeding to the actual incumbency, he would wish him every good fortune. The Senator rose and walked to the door with them, and seemed at a moment ready to ask if—if there was anything else Commander Hopkinson needed?—but he said no more, and they went out into the white sunlight of Santa Fe.

The other boys were excited, wanting all the details, for their own appointments were not by any means certain. When they heard it was only a First Alternate, they shivered for what might befall them, too.

David drove again.

They turned out of town to the south, going home. Hoppy seemed to fall asleep in the front seat beside David. But now and then he would stir slowly. They all felt they couldn't bring him home soon enough. It was a long drive over the pale plains where the sunlight sometimes seemed to waver on the blanching air.

That night, home again, while the other boys stayed at Little Farm with Hoppy, David phoned his mother from the Abbotts' house in town to tell her that the doctor said she must come home.

They reckoned without that quality which long ago in less self-conscious days had been referred to as the Old Fight, of which David Hopkinson, '12, had owned so great a share. After all, there was plenty of visible evidence of it bearing his name in the trophy cases in MacDonough Hall.

The Annapolis entrance examinations were to be given in El Paso in February. Hoppy had every intention of knowing the outcome. If the young candidate from Rio Arriba County failed to pass, David would be the principal. Hoppy now treated himself as cautiously as he had previously been reckless and stubborn. It was a great change for his household to go through.

Little Farm became an invalid's house.

Visitors were rationed. There were few parties, and those were quiet dinners for only a handful of people, all of whom went home early, though not until the prettiest women of the occasion had tiptoed in one at a time to sit on Hoppy's bed, hold his hand, and preserve, while his ironic smile played the truth for them both, the illusion that he was just temporarily out of sorts, and was being very intelligent about how to get back on his feet again.

In all that, Doro was the admiration of everyone. She was ingenious about keeping him occupied and amused. When the snowless winter descended upon them from the great cold heights of air over the plains, bringing harsh sandy winds and a chilling pale blue sunlight, her heart sank.

She could imagine the desolation that was awaiting her.

He was all she had—except, of course, for David, but David would soon be going off to college, either in the Navy or out.

Sometimes when she was alone, she wondered if she could bear for very much longer to watch Hoppy in his painful struggle to see his great project through.

One day when she sat reading to him he interrupted her and said that he had really been a pretty heavy cross for her to bear all these years. Ten years ago, she'd have said to him with a catch of laughter that he was making a transparent play to get her to pet him, and compliment him, and with foolish praise bury his foolish remorse. Not now. His face was deeply sorrowful as he said it. His breath was shallow in his mouth. He reached for her hand humbly. It was the first time in their lives that he'd ever gone so far with any confession.

She was not a good dissembler.

Much as it might hurt them both, she could not help bursting into tears.

They said nothing more about it, but in that melancholy hour, while the wind sang and tugged at the corners of their white wooden house, and the flying sand was drawn in a faint cloud parallel to the plains, they admitted to each other that he was dying, and that if anything might survive him, it would be their love, in its infinite small expressions through the other lives it had touched in many ways.

David was to go to El Paso in February to take the examinations with the other candidates from that region. He was fairly confident of what he knew. Hoppy had been putting him through his paces every afternoon after school making use of all the Naval Academy textbooks he still had or could obtain by mail. There were also specimen examination sheets from previous years which the boy studied until he was letter perfect in them.

Hoppy thought of himself as a great trainer. He knew when to hit it hard, and when to let up.

The night before David was to take the bus to El Paso, Hoppy had Doro give a little supper for their son and some of his friends. Hoppy ordered festive ingredients brought to his bedside and mixed a canister of his dry martinis, making just enough for each of the youngsters to have only one. Doro fed them her celebrated Boeuf à la Stroganoff whose recipe she had learned from a White Russian family in Peking. The young guests tasted the sherry in the sauce and felt sophisticated. After dinner they danced in the front room.

The barking of young male voices, the chatter of young girls, animation and sense of occasion, were too much for Hoppy.

They were all astounded to see him appear suddenly in the doorway from the dining room, wearing a silk scarf, a smart dressing gown with his initials embroidered on the pocket, a pair of evening trousers, black silk socks and patent leather pumps. His hair was shined with tonic and brush.

His eyes sparkled at the sight of young people being so gay and having such fun.

David brought his girl up to speak to Hoppy, and the look he gave her was one that caused her heart to thump, and made every boy in the room seem like a snub-nosed puppy. This was a man, and something of all life, powerful, frightening and desirable, spoke out from him. He was touched at evidence of his effect upon the girl, and a little guilty. He had merely meant to come and look, not to make a pretty high school girl blush. Just the same, he squared his shoulders against his crippling pain, and lingered a little while longer. Then duty assailed him, he said good evening to them all, told Doro to send everyone home, and make David go right to bed.

Hoppy was awake the next morning when David came tiptoeing out to start for the bus station in town on his bicycle. He called the boy, wanting to see how he looked on the first step of his crucial journey. What he saw reassured him. Wisely making no reference to the purpose of the journey, he merely asked David to get for him, if he could find it in El Paso, a bottle of a certain kind of imported British shaving lotion.

The boy came back three days later. He thought he had done well enough, but in any case, there was nothing to be known until they would hear how the principal candidate had fared.

Those weeks until they heard were hard to bear. Hoppy was privately given to spells of cynicism. Politicians were all alike. They remembered only that which would benefit them personally. What could a United States Senator expect to derive from the gratitude or good will of a mortally ill retired naval officer, or his quiet boy? The Mexican vote of Rio Arriba County was something else again. That was what was worth playing to. Life came down to just this, the taste of dust that blew in through the cracks of the windows when the winter twilight was lowering on the plains.

When at last the letter was brought to him by Concha, the maid, franked with the Senator's facsimile signature in blue ink, Hoppy stared at it before opening it.

Here it was.

Whatever it was, it would make all the difference in the world to him.

He felt that he must indeed be weak and pitiably so, for he realized that before opening the envelope, he was streaking through a prayer in his thought; as if it could influence or change the contents of the letter. With smarting eyes, he searched for the place to tear the envelope, and then ripped it open. He read it at a glance, really seeing only the last lines word for word: "—is therefore a pleasure to extend my heartiest congratulations to your son, with every expectation that his career in the service of his country's Navy will be as worthy and distinguished as his father's."

Doro could not hear him, though he was calling her, he thought, rather loudly. When she wandered in a little later to see how he was, he was asleep, clutching the letter. She took it away from him and read. She began to cry, for she knew it was his release. He had "made it." Her heart was heavy to realize that there was nothing now for which he must fight.

He died a few weeks later. The doctors were frank in their amazement that he had held on so long at that. Doro said to them with a betrayal of pride that was almost a rebuke, that they did not know him, then.

She and David decided that they would bury him there, in the Las Vacas Valley.

Wick Thayer could not come as he was at sea with his ship, but Diana came, and Avy and Vivi flew from Pensacola by airline. The Abbotts were helpful.

Hoppy's shroud was his uniform. His dress sword was borne on top of his coffin, which was covered with a flag. They all went from the Episcopal chapel of St. Andrew's, out to the sandy cemetery south of town, which was marked off in the grey plain by a rectangle of precariously rooted cypress trees and lombardy poplars. It was a cold March afternoon. The wind was abroad. A bleak light fell upon all things through a thin white sky. Bitterly enough, the funeral was the only colorful thing in miles. There were mounds of flowers, and about the earthen opening, strips of emerald green straw carpeting intended to resemble grass which would comfort the bereaved with the likeness of a garden rather than a grave. The minister read prayers, and Robert Louis Stevenson's stanza about "Home is the sailor, home from the sea," after which a youthful bugler from the local military academy played taps.

Avy stood by Doro, holding her hand tightly and out of sight among the folds of their overcoats which met by their sides. Her hand trembled so that he could hardly hold it still. He looked sharply at her out of the corner of his eye. But she was standing with her face raised, with—was it possible?— almost a smile over her lips. He flushed with love and admiration for her, and mentally shook his head over both the Millard sisters, one of whom he was lucky enough to have married. Diana, Vivi and David stood in the same line.

A salute was fired by a squad of cadets. The rifles rang in the raw air. Doro gasped at the shock of noise. By pre-arranged agreement, Avy stepped forward, took the sword from the top of the coffin, presented it to David, and stepped back beside Dorothy. The minister handed David a small handful of earth. David knew what he must do. He tossed earth upon the coffin, consigning it and all within it to the dust from which it came and to which it returned. It was a gesture difficult for the son to make; but by its very difficulty, it closed, confirmed and freed in the same moment. They turned away, Avy and David with their arms through Dorothy's, going back to the cars, as the coffin was lowered from sight.

xxi

"Vivi, don't you think we might have one more before we go in to dinner?" asked the Admiral.

Now and then Mrs Grace would weigh such propositions with deliberateness, fingering her platinum chain which had rose diamonds every few inches, and which supported her lorgnon. They watched her, amused, while in abstraction she seemed to be conducting a mental debate over the merits of Avy's suggestion. But then she suddenly smiled, her blue lioness eye brimmed with merriment, and she said that of course they could, as there was just time for one more before they went in. With Commander Morton's help, she went to work refreshing their glasses, while they recalled that half an hour ago she had said the same thing. Diana thought that it was just Vivi's way, of stating terms at any outset, so that everybody would understand her conditions.

"I will never forget," said Diana, "when I took Doro back to

Coronado with me again, after the funeral. She let herself go for the first time in her life, I think. I never saw anyone so tired. She slept all day and all night, practically, for two weeks. She didn't want to see anybody, and I didn't make her—"

"That's where I think you may have been wrong," said Vivi, nodding her opinion at Diana. "People in her condition at such times are not able to judge what is best for them."

Admiral Grace slightly waggled his head and turned to Admiral Thayer.

"You now have a glimpse of what I've had all my life. Vivi never thinks I know what is best for me, at all. Ever. Guess who does?"

"I do," cried Vivi, with a musical quality, her eyes crackling with the light of this endless comedy of marriage in which the husband was both hero and wretch, the wife both heroine and scold.

"She's right, at that," said Avy, ever so mildly, looking at her quizzically.

xxii

Dorothy stayed at Coronado until it was time for David to graduate from high school. She then returned to New Mexico, to close her house for good, packing and crating for still another time all the possessions which in the aggregate symbolized her lifetime with Hoppy. The house was put up for rent, for she would keep it as long as legal residence, to justify David's appointment from New Mexico, seemed the right thing to observe.

In June he reported to the Academy.

She went to Pensacola to visit the Graces for a few weeks.

Florida was warm in summer, but she was dazzled and refreshed by the colors, the ocean, and the youthful society of naval air cadets and their girls which revolved about the Graces (Avy was in command of the station) like an animated garden. She enjoyed acting as a sort of co-hostess for Vivi, at parties when the whole lower floor of the Commandant's Quarters was thrown open, much too big a territory with many too many nooks and crannies, for one woman to look after.

There was a famous morning when the President arrived offshore in the *Houston,* and landed later in the day to inspect the Naval Air Training Station. Flights of single-engined trainers went overhead, passed and repassed, weaving wedges of sound in the blue altitude. After the inspection, the staff escorted him to the Commandant's Quarters to spend a cool half hour in the deep shade of the porch. A drink. Much resonant humor.

They were all fascinated by the range of detailed professional knowledge he revealed in his comments and questions, when they talked shop.

He gleamed at the Millard sisters and said he remembered their father very well, and in fact had at one time used him as an accomplice to convey a White House paper initialled "W.W." from the Secretary of the Navy's office direct to the hands of the Secretary of State without having to go through channels and past too many eyes. He asked if any members of the family were at the Naval Academy now, or were going to be. They were able to give a satisfactory answer to this. He said please, to remember that if either Midshipman Grace or Midshipman Hopkinson ever needed anything he could give them, they were to be sure and not hesitate to drop him a line. He was tanned from much fishing. His eyes were light and brilliant, his teeth were flashingly white. He pinched off his nose-glasses rather often to blink and rub his eyes as if to get rid of the offshore glare, which he faced. Nobody wanted to suggest that they turn his chair for him, since he couldn't do it for himself. He noticed their concern, and indicating his legs, and with a shrug of his shoulders, he asked that someone just shove the back of his chair around a little so he could—there; that was better; that was fine. He gave them all the feeling that there was nothing in the human condition which should embarrass, provided it was acknowledged, and, if need be, corrected. Lighting his own cigarette, he offered Avy one, and then leaned over and held his own light for Avy's.

Doro wrote Diana all about it that evening, and added that she'd had an object lesson in what it meant to face up to things and overcome them. She also said in the letter that after the President had gone back to the *Houston,* one of the officers of the staff said to her that he had always resented, even while he had had to admit, the charm and the power whereby that man had got votes; but that now, after sitting down with him for over an hour (long past the thirty minutes scheduled for the courtesy call), having a drink with him on Avy's porch, where there wasn't anyone who could do a thing of any political value, he'd be damned if he didn't think the whole point was that the man really believed in people.

Two weeks later a flat package came from the White House, containing a signed photograph taken that day in Pensacola.

Dorothy went to Bar Harbor with Vivi in July. She was now able to think about the future. She had been nursing an idea which she talked over with Vivi. She had Hoppy's insurance, but it wouldn't quite keep her by itself. In twenty-four hours, Vivi had plans all written down, and had sent four telegrams for Doro all bearing on her project, which had to do with starting a small bookshop in Coronado, where many of their friends would always be stationed or visiting.

It turned out to be a sound idea, though during the first year she barely made expenses. But the naval establishment in Coronado grew steadily as, during the next few years, affairs looked worse and worse in the Orient. There was a sudden increase of activity. San Diego grew. When Wick was ordered to sea duty, patrolling far Pacific waters, it was plain to Diana that he wouldn't be back soon. She decided to stay in Coronado, help Doro in the bookshop, and still be as near as possible should Wick return to the West Coast for a few days at any time.

It was a suitable arrangement. The shop prospered. Both women enjoyed handling the packages of new books that came in day after day. The shop was almost like a game, instead of a matter of earning a living. They had a great time making the shop as attractive (they said) as a room in somebody's house. Sharing the same comfortable snobberies of taste that spelled good breeding and membership in a knowing society, they accordingly deployed the right kinds of lamps, curtains, chairs and prints in the proper color scheme. They let it get around that good friends of theirs, or of the bookshop, would always find a cup of tea and a watercress sandwich any afternoon after four. In spite of much urging, they resisted the idea that they should expand their activities and open a tea room. They both thought, obscurely, that there was somehow a difference between running a bookshop and a tea room. An eating place. They'd have hated saying it, but they believed it was a difference in ladyship. However, in the face of obvious advantages, they did undertake to add greeting cards, silver boxes of all sizes from Taxco, art reproductions, and Mexican glass to their wares.

It was true that "everyone" did turn up in Coronado sooner or later.

Avy had finished his tour at Pensacola, was now in command of the carrier *Brandywine* and on his way to Pearl Harbor, where Vivi was going to join him.

She came for a week or two at Coronado before sailing from San Francisco. She liked what she found, and she brought pleasant reports of the boys at the Naval Academy. Her own sons were doing creditably. As for David, he was a better than average student, and Doro no doubt knew all about his—an expression which Guinevere Grace detested—his girl-friend. Or did she? Young people were often so odd, about the things they did, and did not, communicate to their parents.

Though she lived to get them, as she said, Dorothy found David's letters curiously disappointing. They were rather flat in tone, precise in word, and indifferent to the kind of detail that made experience live again. She couldn't help contrasting them with Hoppy's letters of long ago, which seemed to make a point of honor of vividness, extravagant humor, ironic exaggeration—anything to make her delight in any extension of his own quality. Perhaps all young people nowadays were different, she thought, excusing David his friendly but unexciting little chronicles that arrived faithfully every week. Perhaps Hoppy's famous disciplines were now having their results. She sighed. Anyhow, it was certain that aside from the obedient reportings of his meagre social activities, which mentioned now this girl, and now that, at dances, or on weekend leaves, there had been nothing that might add up to anything so significant as girl-friend.

xxiv

Vivi had met her, quite by accident, in Washington, at Tommy and Cordelia Richards'. Young Duncan De La Salle Richards was David's roommate, as everyone knew, and in the weekend Vivi had just spent with the Richards, the two boys had come to Washington on leave. That Saturday afternoon, they went to the station to meet a certain train, from which they brought home this girl, who lived in Wilmington.

Her name was Eliza Jenersen. Her father was a surgeon in Wilmington. He was descended from one of the early Swedish families that had settled on the Delaware in the seventeenth century. The girl was tall, as tall as David, even blonder than he, with china blue eyes. She reached out to people with smiling confidence and they responded with whatever best selves they could show.

Vivi reported that Eliza was obviously well-bred, nicely equilibrated between those poles of society which were the despair of modern mothers: on the one hand, a sense that family, and tradition, and manners did matter; and on the other, the slack and slangy unrestraint of all modern offspring, through which girls did their best to look like, sound like, think and drink like boys, who seemed to be more flattered than repelled by such efforts. There was what Vivi and Mrs Richards discussed as a sort of pack psychology. The children ran with *the pack,* and whatever the pack did was all right for them individually to do.

Even in the case of so poised a girl as Eliza Jenersen, there was something odd; for she encouraged both David and Duncan, equally. She did so not in the old way, when everybody could remember girls who quite heartlessly encouraged several men separately and who ended by crushing all hearts but one in the final publication of the victorious suitor's engagement— no, Eliza quite simply took on both David and Duncan, but together, at the same time, as a team, quite openly, and they both seemed to be delighted, said Vivi. The three of them went everywhere together. They dined, went dancing, supping, and ice skating, and to the movies. Duncan told his mother Cordelia Richards that when he and David wrote to Liz, they put their letters in the same envelope, and when she replied, no matter to which of the two she addressed hers, the letter inside always spoke to them both. She was "simply crazy" about them both, and they all laughingly agreed that as a consequence, she could never marry either of them. She was a Catholic. So were the Richardses. Vivi supposed that if any factor gave either of the boys an edge over the other, this would advantage Duncan. Anyway, they both came as near to being in love with her as anybody could, and still preserve the current odd arrangement.

Dorothy was interested in the information, and felt a pang of relief that David was surely a long way off yet from picking out anyone to marry, for nobody could take this Eliza Jenersen affair very seriously, divided as it was in two directions. She wondered why it gave her even the smallest satisfaction to realize that he was not yet really in love. Was she becoming over-possessive? She smiled at such a modern possibility; and yet with every thought, she hugged David to her still, her boy, whose boyhood had in a sense been denied to him and to her; her grown son, who was sworn in his father's footsteps.

Vivi said he was looking very well indeed. He had gained weight; he had a new gravity which, when he smiled, made his expression very appealing; he had talked a good deal about his father, and his discoveries of what Hoppy's position was in the history of the Naval Academy. He seemed awed by this. It was good for him, his Aunt Vivi thought, to realize what he came from, and what he owed everything to. He was sometimes a very puzzling young man. But then, so were her sons. They so often were inclined—all of them—to take the wrong things seriously.

Vivi went on to her domicile at Pearl Harbor, where shortly afterward Avy was promoted to rear-admiral. Vivi, as his consort, was hostess to the middle Pacific Ocean, and—Wick Thayer wrote this to Diana—Neptune would have to learn a thing or two about how to conduct a proper court.

64

Of Eliza, Dorothy heard no word directly from David until the middle of his First Class year. He then wrote her a brief note, saying that she would hear pretty soon from a girl named Eliza Jenersen of Wilmington, Delaware, who was going to marry him, when his time was up, so please to be prepared to hear from her. He was sure she would like Liz. He was sending a photograph of them taken together last summer. Eliza herself would send a more pretentious one, a portrait recently taken in New York. When Dorothy came on for his graduation, she would meet Liz, and Liz's father and mother, who were coming too, of course. Incidentally, he was becoming a Catholic in order to marry her. He wanted his mother's approval and blessing for all these momentous decisions, and sent much love.

Doro was aggrieved at the casual way he disposed of her emotional equity in him, so to speak. What right had the Jenersens to know all this, to give approvals, and make plans for graduation, before she herself had been consulted? But thinking in this direction, she felt mean spirited, and checked such thoughts.

She was pleased with the likeness of Liz when the photograph arrived from her; and her note introducing herself was everything she could have hoped for. It was frank, well-phrased, and generous in the spirit with which it asked for a chance to make Doro accept her. Doro wrote to Liz, and to David, and put her truest self into the letters. After that, letters and telegrams went back and forth more often, as the graduation season approached. She was half-reluctant to go, but she knew the only way she could ever compose her memories was to walk right up to them where they began. There were enough of her own old friends to make this season as pleasant as it might be poignant. Tommy Richards' boy was graduating with David. So was Millard Grace. Avy and Vivi were now back in Washington, where he was assigned to the Navy Department.

They all met the Jenersens for dinner at Carvel Hall in Annapolis, when Midshipman Duncan De La Salle Richards felt called upon to give a June Week dinner party. At first he had thought only to have the young people. Then he hated to leave out David's mother, who was so pretty and so very much interested in them all. But if he asked her, then he would really have to ask Doctor and Mrs Jenersen, and if he did that, why, then, he might as well ask Mill Grace's parents, and for that matter, even his own. That is what he did. He had a private dining room, and cocktails for the old people, and tomato juice, standing up, for the rest of them. A fat lot of chance there was for midshipmen to have a drink, with two admirals and other commencement guests in the room. Anyhow, he sat next to Dorothy at dinner (Vivi asked him if he knew his seating was all wrong) and felt like talking right along to her from the start.

Dorothy had seen him, off and on, through the years of his life, first as a little boy, then a youngster, now a young man. She had always called him Duncan, though David called him "D.D.," pronounced "Deedy," from the initials of Duncan and

66

DeLaSalle, and his mother Cordelia Richards called him Sonny. The latter became his nickname in the service.

Duncan told her that it had all gone along very nicely until a few months ago, just after Christmas, in fact. One evening during study hall, while he was at work on his fourth year math, and doing all right for a change, David had started talking to him in a low voice.

David first of all said that for weeks now he had been getting private letters, separate letters, that was, from Liz, and he couldn't go on much longer without telling Deedy. He said that he and Liz were seriously in love, and considered themselves to be engaged. He guessed it turned into this thing at Thanksgiving time, when she'd been down here for the dance. He'd felt what he could only describe as a stimulating ache. He'd told her about it. She said she had the same thing. In a second, their clever arrangement for three seemed really meaningless, and he and Liz were both miserable over what Deedy might think. All he could say was it was a fact, and nothing at all could change it. To prove how serious he was, he added that he was starting next week to take instruction from the Catholic chaplain so he could be converted and when the time came be ready to marry Liz.

Well! As for Duncan, he assured Dorothy (with a current pun) that she could have knocked him over with a fender. But there was only one thing to do, of course. Confess. He confessed to David that he was practically as bad, because he'd been trying for a long time to figure a way to break up the threesome for the same reason on *his* part, though he had not yet asked Liz if she felt the same way about him. Evidently she wouldn't have.

67

Doro looked down the table at her son, sitting next to Eliza at the far end. The two of them were glowing like the candlelight on the table. She thought that yes, it would wait, successfully. They were like Avy and Vivi—serene, certain, almost calmly the masters of the unknown threats that might rise against their league during such a long engagement. She had a shrewd and rueful thought, to the effect that she and Hoppy could never have survived so long a period of waiting; not with Hoppy as he was.

These graduation days brought back that other June Week for her. She found that she could bear it. It was a peaceful sort of pleasure to see the drills, the parades, go to the afternoon and evening parties of the grownups, and spend the evening of the ball watching from the sidelines, though she danced a few times through the sparkling prismatic colors that were cast across the crowd by the turning mirrored sphere which the Ring Dance Committee had installed overhead.

She found herself smiling with an ache and at the same time a desire to laugh as she watched David and Eliza dancing. They danced almost every dance together. They did not talk much. They didn't seem to need to. They were all by themselves in that great and ceremonial throng. He was in white uniform. She was in a white dress. Their two blonde heads were close. They were spectacular in their beauty, their communion, and their privacy. Everybody spoke of them. They seemed like a dedicated pair, the ideal embodiment, for all the regiment of midshipmen and their girls, of this time of their young lives, and the future which began here tonight, in a ritual that was as significant as it was formless and casual. Doctor Jenersen said he felt like the parent of a sacrificial

68

maiden. A virgin. "Carl!" exclaimed his wife, with a chiding wince, as if he had exposed the family to public view. Well, he replied, he *hoped* so, at least; deliberately missing his wife's bridling point. The dance band drowned the teasing hostilities of the oldsters in a wave of deep brass music. It was a waltz. The youngsters danced with their eyes shut, publicly dreaming. The vast hall pulsed gently with the sum of the illusions celebrated there and then.

xxvi

Perhaps the only moment when Dorothy needed Avy to cling to again was at commencement exercises. But she was sitting between Eliza and Doctor Jenersen. Once again she watched and counted as the names sounded from the stage, and the single file of graduates moved up the carpeted ramp, to salute, shake hands, grasp their commissions, and march down in new freedom and power.

". . . Midshipman Millard Avery Grace . . ."

A couple of rows ahead, Vivi and Avy leaned forward to see their son. A few more names. And then . . .

". . . Midshipman David Warren Hopkinson Junior . . ."

She began to tremble. She saw not only Davie, but Hoppy there, one so fair and one so dark. The moment came back, when she had thought that she was seeing Hoppy for the last time. Who would have expected that so brave a farewell, made so many years ago, still had the power to frighten her all over again? She smiled desperately, and blinked her eyes, watching

David salute so smartly, and put out his right hand so—so cordially, she supposed. He seemed determined, in his brief moment, to put the Undersecretary of the Navy perfectly at ease. She pressed her lips and swallowed, watching David give way to the next graduate, and march down the ramp.

Her own, she thought hungrily.

She had never felt so alone before.

She felt her trembling hand taken and held, with delicate strength, as if to comprehend and to conceal its trembling. She glanced to her right. Eliza held her hand and smiled soberly upon her. Doro gave her one of her shining looks, black and deep. The two really came together in that moment. They never spoke of it.

". . . Midshipman Duncan De La Salle Richards . . ."

He seemed taller than they remembered him, and his hair looked dark red. There was a swagger about him, seen at this distance, which made people smile. He had what amounted to a public personality. It carried. There was heightened applause for him as he passed on his course. For some reason, Eliza blushed as she watched him, and spoke of it later, and said she supposed it was guilty conscience. When it was all over, and time really to say goodbye, Duncan asked David if he could kiss her. David said of course, go ahead and kiss her; all he wanted to be certain of was to have the *last* kiss himself. Much laughter. Much love. Much enthusiastic sadness.

Even those fully adult were something like children, in their private hearts, when the parties were over, and it was time to go back to every day. Even while they recognized that nobody could live forever at such a pitch of sentiment and excitement, they were disappointed when it was all over. Perhaps it was because, though all of the families gathered for graduation would have their own separate occasions and great days—weddings, baptisms, reunions, anniversaries—they would not again, most of them, partake of so grand and so common an event, with such a powerful emotion rising from a whole unified society, as a June Week.

Dorothy returned to Coronado.

xxvii

She didn't come East again until the summertime, two years later, when David was married to Eliza in Wilmington. The Jenersens, as some of the classmates put it, certainly shot the works. The wedding party and the relatives of the groom were put up at the DuPont Wilmington Hotel, where the Jenersens engaged a whole floor.

Duncan Richards was best man.

Eliza had a girl from Philadelphia as her maid of honor, for whom she, and everybody else who was in on the secret, which meant about thirty other young people, strenuously hoped Duncan would fall. Inevitably the result was that after noticing all the symptoms of romantic archness and heavy plotting about him, he took a look at the innocent girl and conceived a calm dislike for her. He remarked to someone that it was a pity, but every woman had something of the procuress in her, even his darling Eliza, with her plot.

Everything else, however, went off well. Dorothy gave the bride and groom a small convertible roadster. Duncan was in charge of it, and determined that there should be no vulgar nonsense about signs, old shoes, and other tribal obscenities (as he said) to embarrass the bridal pair. He arranged to drive the bride and groom away from the reception to the station, where, he said, they were to hurry to their drawing room on the Boston day train that went through at two-fourteen. It was a secret which he let slip here and there, as if he were amiably confidential through too much champagne. He whispered it around that it would be fun if there was a crowd down at the station well ahead of them, so that when he drove up with them, there would be what a reception! Those of a mind to take part slipped slyly away ahead of the bride and groom.

Accordingly there was nobody to bother them when Duncan took David and Eliza to Doctor Jenersen's own car, put them in, and drove them not to the railroad tracks but to a filling station in the country on the Chadds Ford road, where they found the new car, with the top down, and a little square envelope tied to the steering wheel with a note from Dorothy inside.

It was a surprise, and a successful one. They were safe from intrusion by their well-wishers. Eliza and David were breathless with excitement over the car. They insisted that Duncan—"Deedy"—get in, and drive down the road to a tavern, where they could all have one last glass of beer together. He protested that they would want to be on their way, alone. Nonsense. They only wished he could go with them. He blushed with love and said the only way to get rid of them was to agree. They drove off, the new car twinkling and virtually soundless in the August sunshine.

To see how happy they were was almost as good as getting

married himself, Duncan declared. David was the handsomest, strongest, truest man he knew. Eliza was the prettiest, sweetest girl and he, Duncan, would always love her. He felt almost proprietary about them and their union, as if he had invented it. When they brought him back to the filling station, he hugged them both, seeing how longingly they both tore themselves away from him, so that it was almost with consoling words that he sent them off.

He drove back to the wedding house, where they were just putting the Bishop into his limousine. Duncan found Dorothy and said goodbye to her with an impulsive kiss, hoped he would be stationed in Coronado soon so he could see her, and then went off with a crowd of the bachelor ushers who promised to raise hell all night in Philadelphia, for which, after this much of a start on liquor, and high feeling, and vicarious love, they all felt good and ready.

xxviii

The honeymoon was three weeks long, spent in wandering throughout New England.

At the end of that time, David was ordered to Coronado. They couldn't believe their luck. Dorothy wrote of her happiness. The young couple drove West in the car. She had a little house all waiting for them. Beyond renting it for them—which took effort, for certain naval activities were increasing in volume and there was little to be had—she did nothing to the house, knowing how much they would enjoy furnishing it for

73

themselves. They moved in, living on love, laughter and orange crates, as they put it. It wasn't long till things they bought began to arrive. They hardly had time to be respectable for their first dinner party, before David was ordered to sea in the destroyer *Mornington,* which was proceeding to Philippine waters.

Eliza, a full-fledged Navy wife, now knew what it meant to settle down in the port nearest to the scene of her husband's duty, however far away it might be; and wait till he might come ashore again.

She had news from him every few days by air mail right up until December, 1941.

On the Sunday of the seventh, she was lunching with Doro and Diana Thayer and heard the disastrous radio news with them. She thanked God she was with them at that time. It was not known where Wick's cruiser squadron was, or exactly where the *Mornington* was. Eliza took heart from watching Diana's face as hour after hour brought more fearful intimations of ruin and loss of the men of the Army and the Navy at Pearl Harbor and in the Philippines. In Diana's expression there was no pretense that things weren't as bad as they were. But there was the most grounded courage showing there, for no matter what the news might eventually bring to her in personal terms, it was what her lifetime with Wick had meant to prepare her for professionally. They all lived with an admission that it was for times like these that they had been educated, tempered and confirmed. Let them be equal to it. Eliza saw that the older women were. All this without thought; automatic and true to their characters. Her inexperienced heart struggled to be as worthy.

74

Perhaps, they all said later, those first weeks were the most unbearable; though of course, they were borne, and so were the years that followed. But news of any sort took forever to come. When at last they heard something, it was not good. They heard that David had been wounded in the attack on Manila on the eighth. How badly, they could not discover.

There was no news for a long time as to what had befallen the *Mornington*.

When Manila was evacuated, the news of that reached Eliza and Doro oddly on the day when they had brief letters from David, written from the Navy hospital in Manila, saying that he was better, had been wounded in the back, was now walking a little, and they would be disgusted if they could see how much weight he was gaining lying around and doing nothing. His only reference to the war was that things were rugged. He would write again soon. But they could see, couldn't they, that he must be improving, as this was his own handwriting? They speculated as to whether he was protesting too much.

They were anxious for weeks to find out what had happened to him after Manila was abandoned. Their hopes rose when they found out that he had been removed to Corregidor; and then sank lower by the day, as the siege of the island fortress drew closer and closer to what could only be its degrading end.

It seemed that each new event called upon Doro and Eliza to make yet another compromise with life and sorrow in David's name. First, he had been only wounded; how much better than if he'd been killed! Next, he'd been transferred to Corregidor; how much better than if he'd been left in Manila! Then, Corregidor fell, and all besieged forces there were taken prisoner; how much better than if they all died, David included, of a starvation siege!

If he was a prisoner, then he was at least alive. If he lived, there was still a future.

How could they get any news? The Navy couldn't say. Two months after the fall of the Philippines, a list was released. Lt. (j.g.) David W. Hopkinson, Jr. was "missing." What could that mean? It might mean that he was dead, but without official proof. It might mean that he had escaped, and word would come any day. Perhaps he was among those who were making their way southward, night by night, and would eventually reach— There were many possibilities. They reviewed them all. The one thing they refused to admit, even in their innermost thoughts, was that he might be gone from them forever, son and lover.

Their certainty was a power. It helped others in the same plight. They both—Doro and Eliza—worked in the bookshop, and spelled each other at the Red Cross. Diana returned to Washington for the duration. She saw that there was not enough for three of them to do in the shop and, realists, all of them, they saw no point to inventing tasks to keep busy. Eliza and Doro drew closer to each other. They said silently to one another, that the world, the Navy, the Western Union, might all think the worse could have happened to David; they, the two of them, were convinced that he was not lost to them.

76

XXX

It was one year and four months before there was any further direct word from him; and then one day in Coronado, Eliza received a postcard through the international Red Cross, saying, in his own writing, that he was "well and busy; all love."

It was undated; it was meagre enough; but they fed on it. Their spirits rose. No matter how long ago it may have been written, it was the truth at the time, and it must still be true.

Their friends said Doro and Eliza were remarkable, the way they bore up. Somehow the strain of not knowing must actually be worse, everyone said privately, than knowing the worst and having it horribly and heartbreakingly over with. Untactful but helpful individuals now and then hinted such a sentiment in talking to Doro. She was always deeply angry for a second or two; then she would recover herself, and realize that they were trying to be helpful. But what, she asked herself, could they know of love, who talked that way? What sacrifice and what suffering, even this heavy lump beside her heart, would she not bear if only it prove its faith, and let God bring him safely home again whenever it might be possible?

She was tried—so was Eliza—by drift of rumor and human relish for bad news.

There was a young man, an ensign, who got away from a Japanese prison camp in the Philippines. In some obscure way, the possibility was suggested that David had been seen with him.

What was his name? How could he be reached, for further

77

information? He was a cousin of my friend's husband, and I will write and find out more for you. Weeks of waiting while that was going on. Eventually a reply giving the name, and adding that though it was believed out here that he had managed to get away, with two other prisoners, they could get nothing official on it.

They took the name, and followed it up through the Navy Department, which reported in a few days that there was no official record of any such information.

And so for a few months, Doro and Eliza believed that David was free, and making his way southwestward by whatever prodigies of adventure, tenacity and wit he could command. He was strong. They knew that. He was clever. People liked him at once, and trusted him. There would be plenty of natives who would be glad to help him. May he sleep safely tonight. Not in the cold tropical rain. Sleep well, my darling. Everything is safe. Everything is all right. Now that I am alone, I can admit that my heart hurts not just when I think of it, but now, and at every minute, and all the time.

Then they received a postcard, another prisoner message. "Studying Spanish, learning fast. Am o.k." What did this mean? Did he not get away? Did he get away after it had been written? One day it would seem depressing and hopeless news. Another day it would seem reassuring.

Cordelia Richards heard from her husband who was out in the Pacific that a man had escaped from a prison camp, and that he had brought news of a number of deaths among the Americans there. The chaplain had died, and so had twenty or thirty others. The man had carefully written all the names down, but had lost the list in his travels, but he could remember most of them. Asked if Hopkinson were among those, the man thought a moment, and then said he believed so. He was afraid so. There were only two names beginning with H, and one of them was short, Hicks, it was, and the other was a long name like Hopkinson, and that was what it was. Admiral Richards in his letter said of course this was not official, and there might still be some slim chance of error, so Cordelia had better do as she thought best about telling Doro and Eliza. It would be a dreadful thing to give a wrong report about a thing like that; still, everybody knew how hungry Doro and Eliza were for information.

Mrs Richards couldn't make up her mind to tell them. But she thought she would play safe. She asked Diana Thayer, in Washington, what she would do about it if she were in that situation. Diana said to do nothing. Tommy Richards was right. If there was a chance of error, the best thing was to say nothing. Had she told anybody else? Hardly anybody, said Cordelia. Well, it was too bad to've told anyone at all, but from now on, it would be best not to mention it.

But Cordelia's "hardly anybody" told enough other people, so that in a few days, the rumor had travelled from Washington to Coronado, where Doro's friends heard it. It was not long until, acting in perfectly good heart, someone called her up and said it was heartbreaking news, and just wanted her to know that everybody was thinking of her, and was there anything at all anybody could do for her or Eliza?

Such dances of death were more cruel to endure than the small facts with which they lived.

They made periodical appeals to the Navy Department,

every time a new rumor, or false hope, turned up; but each time all the Navy Department could say was, "Missing."

The time at last came when the Allied forces were moving back into the Philippines.

Shortly before the liberation of Manila, three Japanese prison ships were known to have moved out, presumably loaded with American prisoners for transfer to other Japanese held territory. Insufficiently informed as to the purpose of the ships, United States submarines torpedoed and sank them in Manila Bay. Few Americans on board survived. It was officially authenticated that as the ships were sinking, and men were struggling in the water, Japanese sailors on the ships machine-gunned and grenaded them. Out of one ship's cargo of over seven hundred prisoners, only four were known to have survived. Losses were almost as great on the other two. A United States naval officer who managed to swim ashore, elude the retreating Japanese, and join an American column many days later, gave an account of the accident and the atrocity. Among those whom he had positively identified in the water near where his ship had gone down was Lt. (j.g.) D. W. Hopkinson, Jr., whom he knew because they had served together on board the *Mornington*.

He remembered calling to Hopkinson to swim over his way, so they could strike out for shore together. But a sweep of machine gun bullets came their way from the deck of another sinking prison ship, and he had had to dive under the water. When he came up again, he had lost Hopkinson, and though he called, there was no answer. He had started swimming then for land.

There was no need for the listeners to dwell in their thoughts upon the various ironies implicit in such information. Still another time had they been tantalized by hope and despair.

A few weeks later, they received a visit from the young officer who had reported on the sinkings. He was able to tell them that David as far as he knew had been in pretty good health. They had not been on the same prison ship, or even in the same prison compound, and all he had to go on was that brief glimpse, in the water, that afternoon. He thought David looked pretty thin, but to tell the truth he was surprised to see him at all, for when he had last seen him in hospital before Manila was lost in 1942, it had seemed that David would never survive his wounds, which had been very serious. Evidently he had recovered the use of his arm, for he was certainly swimming with both arms that afternoon in the Bay.

This was more than they had ever known before, in detail, and they stored it away to be thought over afterward, in misery that must yet make opportunities for consolation and reassurance—the endless process of their waking days. If he had been so badly wounded, and had recovered enough to swim, even though it must have seemed at one time as though he would never use one of his arms again, why, then, that must surely mean that his naturally strong constitution was helping him to endure whatever— He had always been a superb swimmer, and given any chance to swim at all, there would be no doubt that he— If a fellow as frail looking as this officer who was telling all about it could come through a thing like that, then David, with his vitality—

Their thoughts were like little trapped creatures, dashing in any direction, whether there was hope of escape or not.

81

They asked the visiting officer about conditions in the camps?

He looked sick, for a moment, and with a change of thought which they could see in his eyes, he said they weren't good, of course, but then again, they weren't too bad. But they knew he was lying, and they blessed him for it in their minds, for their valor was worn so thin by this time that now and then almost a giddiness seized them, and their cheerfulness became a condition of survival itself. In nightmare, it was as if they could say to the world, see, here is my little monster of anguish. Isn't it cunning?—for it had become so familiar a part of them that short of loathing themselves, they could not loathe it really.

xxxi

In June of that summer, the last summer of the war, Admiral Grace returned to the United States for two weeks of conferences in Washington. He made a point of stopping alone in San Diego to see Dorothy and Eliza.

They were all shocked at each other's looks.

Avy was thin and drawn, under his deep tan. He had been at Okinawa with his carriers. The kamikazes were bad beyond anybody's knowledge. He believed we were "nearing the end of it all, though." This trip had "something to do with that."

He thought the two women were much thinner. He could report no signs of their cracking up. He felt that maybe just a little bit of a cracking up would be good for them both. He took them out to dine. His quiet waggeries touched them deeply.

He was sure. He was affirmative. In his face there was admission of how bad trouble could be, where he came from. In everything he said and communicated otherwise there was an empowering belief, a certainty, that we would "make it"; and by that was meant not only the war, for on that subject he never had a doubt of any kind since the Battle of the Coral Sea, when he had commanded the action that had turned the Japanese back from the threat to Australia, and thus had helped to start the grand turn of the tide, at sea, in the air, and on land.

They told him what they knew. He said he would personally make inquiries when he got to Washington. He gave them both a humorously gallant kiss, and said they'd hear from him very soon. His plane was waiting. It was time he was in the air.

Whether it was because of his inquiries or not, was never clear. But a few weeks later, after he had returned to the far Western Pacific, there was official notification that David was safe. He was a prisoner still, somewhere in Japan. The list came out through the Red Cross. Duncan Richards was in the same camp, after being listed as missing for three months, following the loss of his destroyer escort between Saipan and Okinawa.

They remembered Avy's feeling about the end of the war. It couldn't be long now. David was safe. Eliza felt she could leave Dorothy and go East to stay with her family for a little while. They couldn't say to each other what they felt. They couldn't even define it for themselves. It shone in their eyes.

Within a very few weeks, the Japanese surrender came.

Hardly a fortnight later, official notification arrived that Lt.

(j.g.) David W. Hopkinson, Jr. had died a prisoner in Japan five days before cessation of hostilities.

There was no news beyond the bald statement.

But Duncan Richards had been repatriated in early autumn, to a hospital in the United States. He was well enough to go home to visit his parents, who were stationed at Annapolis, in January. He would be able to tell whatever there was to know about David's last days.

xxxii

Commander Morton had not expected to stay for dinner, but Mrs Grace did not have to urge him. However, he hoped she wouldn't mind if he would just eat and run, because he was expecting a certain Miss Sarah Cleveland to arrive some time after dinner to spend the weekend with his mother and himself, and he should be there to receive her.

"If you really feel you must," said Vivi, as they were all finishing their coffee in the Brazil room.

"I really do, Mrs Grace. It's been terribly nice."

"We're glad you could stay. You're sure you won't just wait till Eliza arrives?"

Admiral Grace saw the small struggle that was going on within his aide.

"Let him go, Vivi," he declared. "He don't want to risk offending you because of your three stars, but he's got a girl coming, and he don't want to risk losing whatever he might risk losing by making her mad at him."

Morton laughed gratefully, and relished the Admiral's deliberate bad grammar, like that of an eighteenth century lord.

"Very well," said Vivi, "I'll stop hazing you. But you must bring her to Chapel in the morning, and then back here afterward before lunch. I won't keep you for lunch. But you do have to bring your young women here for me to see, if I'm to look out for you. If I'm not satisfied then I shall simply tell you so. Not but what I'm sure your young women are all most eligible. What is your Miss Cleveland like?"

"Oh, she's tall and very goodlooking, and knows everybody in the world, and is very clever. —I like her very much," he added, hoping to indicate that while he liked her, he was not in love and was not necessarily pursuing Miss Cleveland with matrimony in mind, as Mrs Grace had apparently concluded on the smallest evidence. Why else her talk about approval and eligibility?

"What does she do?" asked Vivi.

"Vivi, let him go," said Avy with a comic groan.

"Oh, she writes rather well, and plays the piano extremely well, sort of slangily, you know, but she knows all the modern music, serious and popular."

"I believe I must have seen her picture here and there."

"Oh, I think so," said Phil.

"Well, run along."

He thanked her again, and said he would certainly bring Sarah to Chapel and over here afterward. The Admiral got up and saw Morton to the head of the stairs. Then he came back, and said there was no telling when Eliza might be rolling in with young Richards. He believed he would just go up to bed, read a little while, and then go to sleep. If Eliza arrived before his light was out, and if they would let him know, he would get up to greet her. Otherwise he would see her in the morning. He hoped Wick and Diana wouldn't mind if he left them now.

Not at all. Wick wanted to go over and see Tom Richards for a little while. Diana and Vivi had much to catch up on. Diana would work on her Braille punching machine. Whenever she had a chance she made editions of books for the blind, much as other women knitted or sewed.

Well. In that case: Admiral Grace patted his blue coat just below his ribs at each side, and teetered once or twice on his small feet, and left them with one of his red, white and blue smiles.

"Avy," murmured his wife, thinking about him after he'd gone. She was in a little abstraction which made the Thayers glance at one another; knowing how lovingly she measured all he had brought her, and how clearly she knew just how much she had brought him; and how still after these many years, she was fascinated by him, for those little deeps of trivial mystery she found in him, and had never been able to plumb.

"So if you would excuse me, too," said Wick, rising, "believe I will go see Tom for a while. —I won't be late," he added to Diana.

"We'll wait for Eliza," said Vivi.

"Poor darling," said Diana.

"She and Doro will be good for each other," said Wick.

"I think it was kind of you both to come here so you could be with them," said Vivi.

"It was Wick's idea. The minute he heard, he said we had to come. I wanted to, terribly," said Diana.

"You realize, of course," declared Vivi, her eyes betraying that energy which she could summon at any time for the purpose of giving design to affairs, "that we're going right through the day as if nothing on earth were the matter. We do have these rather momentous Sundays here. I think it will do both Doro and Eliza much good to have things to do beyond themselves. For a little while, anyway. Then when they may want to, we can settle down to make plans with them."

"Do I have to go to Chapel, Vivi?" asked Wick, with the plaintiveness of a child.

"You most certainly do," she replied, chiding him for his joke even as she acknowledged it.

"He'll survive it," said Diana. "Go on, go to Tom's. Give Cordelia my love. I don't know if I can ever face her, she's such a fool, the way she let that story get around about David. Not that it matters now, of course."

"My dear, it always matters," said Vivi; "insensitivity will always show, in a thousand ways. I'm devoted to Cordelia. We get along splendidly. I never listen to what she is saying."

"Well, now that you are both safely launched upon your woman's work," said Wick, "I guess I can leave you."

He touched his wife's cheek with the back of his hand, walked neatly over to Vivi with little steps, bent down and kissed her on the ear, and then strode briskly to the hall, down the stairs, and after picking up his cap and gloves from the billiard table in the room off the downstairs foyer, let himself out the door on to the driveway.

It was a misty evening. Admiral Thayer was chilly without his topcoat, but the air tasted cold and sweet when he took it in deep breaths. He remembered fairly recent times in the South-

87

west Pacific when all he had wished for was to be cold once again; really cold, with chattering teeth and shivers. This quiet mild damp cold was a luxury to him. He decided to stroll a few minutes instead of crossing directly over Buchanan Road from Avy's house to Admiral Richards' house. The lights on the grounds were like lanterns, blooming through the heavy air. Bancroft Hall was honeycombed with lights. The mist distorted the rows of lighted windows and made them seem to be smaller than they really were, and farther away, and the building to be a luminous fantasy, higher than he had remembered it.

Or was it really the mist in the air tonight that gave him this impression?

Perhaps the years had altered his memory.

He walked toward the great building. How much he remembered of its life; how much of his own life was threaded directly to it. He prided himself on not being a sentimental alumnus, the kind who returned to the scene of his youth in an orgy of self-pity to seek the mournful joy of what was forever gone. Yet this place was part of him. He didn't want to go back, certainly. But he could remember sharply the terms of his life here so long ago, how much they had taught him, and how much they had not taught him.

He paused and stared up at the window in the pale stone walls.

It was Saturday night, before taps. Free time. He could hear radios, phonographs, and that American musical texture in the air of many young men whistling at random, each happy with his own melody, none hearing the other's, and all content. It made him smile. Some of them would be polishing things.

Some writing letters. Some reading. Some studying—but not many, on Saturday night. Some gossiping. Somewhere, somebody drawing pictures for The Log or The Lucky Bag. Some taking showers, standing dreamily, absently, in the warm rain of the bath, content with their animal manhood. Vessels of duty, all of them, since that was what it was all about. Beyond that, he wondered what it was that they all had in common, professionally and personally, at that time of their lives, and in that place. He supposed, looking up at the lighted windows and strolling on toward the cutter sheds at the near end of Dewey Basin, that it was self-fulness. By that he meant preoccupation with themselves, which was natural; but to the exclusion of what other people, other men, were really like. Once you got the sense of what another man was really like, what all the men in your command were made of, and how their feelings were likely to run, why, then you never afterward felt quite the same about the commands you gave, and the conditions you took for granted, and the arbitrary professional views you inherited about the subject of mankind as machinery.

He went on to the end of the walk and looked out over the Severn. It was pitch dark, except for a tiny glowing light or two about the old moored training ships to his right. He turned back and looked at all of the buildings he could identify from their lights. A hardy emotion clambered alive in him, as if to take flight on wings that strove heavily to be free. In the war so lately ended, the battles so recently finished and won, he had many times been in the midst of death. The men of his command had paid heavily for the victories of the fleet. He had loved them living, dying, and dead. Together, they had all

89

done what had to be done. Nobody had the smallest notion of what it would be like, of what it was like, until they met it head on in battle. Here, tonight, he stood in the midst of this simple Saturday night, and the youngsters were whistling away, and taps would sound pretty soon, and in the background, the basements, the engine rooms, the power plants, the lighted windows, the looming dome of the chapel, the guard offices, the headquarters switchboard, all over the grounds, there hovered that innocent energy whose purpose was to train young men for command, for defense, and for battle if need be. He felt a turn of thought. Very well. He could not dismiss it with a swallow. This was his first time back since the day of his graduation. He supposed what was struggling to come free in him was a sort of blessing, almost a prayerful hope for those brisk and ignorant lives that momentarily inhabited the Academy and gave it its point. He felt like some classical warrior returned to his tribe after a clash of arms in distant places, with a benediction for the young warriors still at home that would carry wisdom and protection to them, out of his knowledge of how things were when the enemy's blood beat for yours.

The intensity of his feeling was surprising to him. He did indeed feel delivered. His spirits rose. He smiled to the darkness and nodded his head, and said to himself that it was really wonderful, how the wives could sit down, as no men did, and talk things over, and unsnarl all the things that had been wound up inside them, and straighten them out, sounding sensible and experienced all the while, and never for a moment losing sight or control of the immediate present during the process. Ordinarily he did not consider himself a thoughtful man. Stocky and muscular, of a steady humor, he unself-consciously believed himself to be a man of action, as if such a classification would exclude the other. He was a little embarrassed by his storm of sentiment; yet he disdained to deny it or shrug it away as some might have done. He simply nodded, confirming what it had clarified for him, and strolled up the walk again to Admiral Richards' house. The porch light was on. It had a look of expectancy about it. Wondering if it was for him, he rang the bell.

xxxiii

Cordelia Richards answered the door herself, and at once explained that she had let everybody go; it seemed so pointless to keep the houseboy here this late, just to answer the door, when nobody was expected but Duncan, but it was, she added, simply divine to see Wicklow Thayer. She turned and called over her shoulder to her husband.

"Tom, here's Wicklow Thayer, looking simply divine. —It wasn't Sonny," she added, in case her husband didn't understand. Then, as she always did after her frequently superfluous actions, she laughed and spread her right hand on her breast, and shared the joke on herself with the nearest person.

She took Wick to the sun porch which served the Richardses as their habitual living room. Admiral Richards rose and came to meet them, and wrung Wick's hand with many exclamations of surprise and pleasure. Each explained what he was doing here (Admiral Richards was writing a report on officer training methods, and had returned here for the purpose), and assured the other that that was perfectly fine. Cordelia mixed them something to drink, and asked how Diana was, and sent her messages, and received those which Wick had for her. Then she said, with a look at her husband which was so searching and hopeless that it gave Wick something of a pang, that they didn't know what in the world to make of Sonny, their son Duncan, since he had come home to stay with them for a little while.

Wick said he supposed that the prison camp experience was probably responsible for whatever it was.

Yes, Mrs Richards thought there was obviously some perfectly good explanation for it.

"But that doesn't make it any pleasanter to go through."

"Oh, come on, now, dearie," said Tom Richards patiently, "you'll have Wick thinking—"

"Oh, no, not at all," she hastened to say. "It's just that Sonny won't talk to us. He doesn't want to talk simply in general. At all."

Maybe he's just grown up enough to decide to behave exactly as he wants to, thought Wick. I should think plenty of times it would be pleasant not to say a word. Or listen to one, for that matter.

They got off the subject. Tom and Wick began to exchange news. It was not long until Cordelia had an impulse to turn on the radio, which conversation always made her feel like doing. She travelled the networks with her dial, shopping around and humming, and then finally left it tuned to a program made up wholly of insults exchanged by two comedians except for such moments as they spent in joining one another to insult an absent third comedian famous for his own program. The merry dialogue was broken by crashes of audience laughter, applause and whistling. Mrs Richards turned toward the radio and smiled at it whenever she enjoyed one of the wisecracks. She had never got over the impression that it was a two-way instrument. Working on a piece of needlepoint, she had the illusion that she was hearing every word the men with her were saying, as well as listening to the show.

Presently they heard heavy footsteps coming over the front porch.

"Sonny!" exclaimed Cordelia.

She left her chair to go to meet him. In a moment she brought him back.

"You remember Admiral Thayer, Sonny? We've been stationed with them so often?"

Wick held out his hand, and the young man shook it. Duncan didn't speak, but he smiled and nodded. His face was pale. His red hair looked fiery and coarse, clipped short as it was. He no longer seemed particularly underweight. His eyes were deep under his brows, shadowed by them, and darkened by an habitual frown. A distant light lurked in them, as if they were windows in a dark house, far within which burning lanterns were now and then carried from room to room, on some mysterious search. His big mouth was framed by deep furrows. The habitual expression of his face now seemed to be one of quiet bitterness. In contrast, when he smiled, the effect was extraordinary, for his white, sober face broke into an expression of such warmth of feeling that he seemed like another man; and you wondered how two such characters could inhabit the same young body.

His mother gave him a highball, which he began to drink

93

indifferently with rapid and regular little sips. Cordelia chattered.

"Well. Did you bring Eliza down from Wilmington with you?"

"Yes."

"I suppose you took her to the Graces."

"Yes."

"How is she?"

"She's fine."

"That's good. Is she going to stay long?"

"I don't know. Nothing's settled."

"I suppose she came mainly to see Doro?"

"That's right."

"Did you have a nice time in Wilmington? What did you do?"

"Very nice. Mostly talked to Liz. We did go out once or twice."

"How are the Jenersens?"

"They're fine."

"I always thought *she* was such a pretty little thing."

"She still is."

There was a brief silence. Cordelia looked at Wick and shrugged at him with shoulder and brow, as if to say, You see what I mean?

Duncan saw her do it, and closed his eyes a second and rubbed them, smiling into his hand. His father regarded him with a fond and puzzled view. He thought the boy would come out of it all right; he was so much better than when he first got home. He was all for leaving him alone.

"Well," said Wick, standing. "I think it's time for me to run along. We'll see you all tomorrow, I imagine."

"Oh yes. We're coming over after Chapel to see Doro."

"Good."

"Admiral Thayer, I'd like to walk across the street with you, sir, if I may?" said Duncan.

"Delighted, sir."

Cordelia and Tom, though pleased at this surge of interest, were a trifle nettled at its going out of the family, so to speak.

Once outside, young Richards didn't say anything at all. They crossed the lawns and the pavement of Buchanan Road, and came to the stoop at the front of the Superintendent's Quarters. It was now really cold. The mist hung in heavy veils about all the lights of the grounds, and draped the dark bulk of the buildings, sweeping them to earth in insubstantial folds. The chapel loomed beyond where they stood.

"Is there anything you want me to do for you, son?" asked Wick.

"Well, I guess not, after all. I just thought."

He stopped and seemed to find some refuge in the dead silence. Wick let him alone, and stood on the lowest step of the house as if in perfect comfort, with all the time in the world. He'd stand there as long as this tall young man with something on his mind didn't go home of his own volition.

"Well," said Duncan finally, "I went up to Wilmington to see Liza. I went because I knew I had to tell her all about it. I was there with David at the last. I saw him every day. I was with him and the chaplain when he died. We had the same thing to go through. I knew Liza would want every bit of it. So I had to tell her. She insisted on asking about everything. I

95

tried at first to make her think it was better than it was, but she was too real and too smart for that. I watched her very carefully to see just what I must stop doing that hurt her. But I might as well have saved my efforts. She made me give it all. I never did anything harder in my life. I used to think years ago when we were here at the Academy that I was in love with her, and when David married her I staged a colossal binge in Philadelphia because of what I had missed out on. Nuts. I didn't know a thing about it. What it really is, I mean. I want to marry her, more than ever, all over again. But Lord, how differently I feel about it."

Silence.

Duncan lighted a cigarette. Admiral Thayer decided to risk a question.

"How does she feel about it?"

"Far's I can tell, pretty much my way. But you know how it is. She's thinking of Mrs Hopkinson. Liza wouldn't feel like doing anything about it right away, even if I came right out with it. —How do you think I am, sir?"

"What do you mean?"

"I mean, do you think I'm—I'm well enough to be thinking along the lines I'm thinking along?"

The poor doubtful question gave Wick a turn under his heart.

"Why, I hadn't thought anything about it, one way or the other, to tell you the truth."

Duncan exhaled his cigarette smoke with a fume of relief. Wick could not possibly have reassured him more genuinely.

"Have you seen Liza lately, sir?"

"Oh no. Not since just before the war, when they were at

Coronado, and I put in for a few days. They had Diana and me to dinner, with Doro. I remember we drank a toast to you."

"You *did?* Who proposed it."

"Why, as I recall, it was David."

"David, eh? God damn it, he would do it. He was the best friend anybody ever had."

"Yes. I knew his father just about as well."

"Yes. Then you know his mother too?"

"Oh yes."

"So do I."

They spoke these simplicities so fondly that each knew the depth of the other's feeling.

Another long silence.

Then Duncan, with what sounded like a smiling voice, said,

"Well, good night, Admiral. I've certainly been glad to talk with you."

"Good night, my boy. Certainly wish you the best of luck on all that."

"It sounds all right to you, then?"

"Why. Good Lord, I don't know that I even ought to vote."

"No, I suppose not. It's something for me to. Anyway, I haven't said anything to anybody else yet about it. Except Liza, and then not right straight out."

"But you have a feeling she knows, eh?"

"Oh, she knows."

"I see. Well, see you tomorrow, son. Good night."

"Good night, sir. —Tell her good night again, for me."

"Won't you come in, for a night cap, or something?"

"Oh, no, thank you, sir. I'm not drinking much."

"Very well. I'll tell her. Good night."

97

"Good night, Admiral."

Wick went up the steps, and then at the door, turned to look after the figure retreating through the fog to the house across the street. Until he passed it, the street lamp across the street printed the shadow of young Duncan Richards on the mist, a larger, ghostly image of him, like the very doubts, memories, and hopes that animated his real being.

xxxiv

Wick let himself into the house, and at once heard their voices and saw the warm light coming from the library. He went to join them there.

He found Eliza Hopkinson just saying good night to Diana and Vivi. She kissed them on the cheek and then he kissed hers. He held her off to look at her, and her china blue eyes seemed to him as young as ever. But the rest of her told him another story. She was thin, and rather pale, there was a sort of excruciating tired sweetness about her mouth. She had a faintly breathy tone to her voice which confessed her dead-tiredness, not from physical effort, but from years of telling herself every courageous lie she could think of; and from the past five months of admitting to herself that David was really gone, this time forever.

"You look mighty sweet, honey child," declared Wick, like a proper Mississippian.

"I've been hearing all about you, and Uncle Avy," she replied. "I'm so proud."

She was still just about the prettiest girl he knew. She was not in mourning. She wore a tweed suit and a piece of fur, and held a fur coat over her arm. Somebody, probably Duncan, had given her a flower, and she had it pinned to her lapel.

"Now I'm going up. I'll see everybody in the morning. I want to be down when Doro arrives."

"I'll take you up," said Vivi. "I believe Duncan Richards took all your bags up. Is there anything else?"

"I put an armful of new books in the hall. I want you to take your choice. I still read every night before I can sleep. Before going to sleep. Good night," she added to the Thayers. Vivi led her to the hallway and upstairs.

"Well," said Wick, settling down with a cigarette, "she seems rather done in. Except that there's a light in her eye, isn't there?"

"There certainly is. She's marvellous. —What do you mean?" said Diana, appraising him with a calculating wonder.

"Oh, nothing. It's just that there's something about her that I think at any other time or under any other circumstances you'd call an air of sort of happiness."

"Why *Wick!*"

"Maybe I imagine it."

"Oh, I don't know." It was too interesting to dismiss summarily. "Have you heard anything?"

"Not in the usual sense. But when I left Tom and Cordelia, their boy, Duncan, followed me outside."

"Oh. He did! —He was here for a few minutes. I thought he was still sort of badly off. Did you?"

"I did till he got to talking. He's all right, really. He's just got it bad."

"Got it bad?"

"Mm. You remember he was supposed to be in love with Liza once?"

"Yes, of course, but that was just that silly thing they all three had fun with. What'd he say?"

"Said he was crazy to marry her."

"Well! —Of course, they've always been devoted, if not in love."

"Love," said Wick flatly. "Right now."

"I wonder if she—"

"Absolutely. At least the boy thinks so. But then in his state, a lot of things might look like things to him."

Diana soberly regarded her husband. He smiled privately at the kind of almost professional excitement a love affair began to stir up in any woman who heard about it. He wondered if he had done the young people wrong in mentioning the matter to anyone, even his wife, who was so fascinated by his information that she was staring right at him without seeing him at all, he was sure. Her white face, with its red peony lipstick, her dark eyes behind her heavily-rimmed working glasses, her white hand with its forgotten, long-ashed cigarette, tickled him. He leaned suddenly forward, put his hand on her knee, and said,

"Diny, honey, maybe I should never have mentioned it. I may be all wrong."

"W. B. Thayer," she said, like a stranger, "I'd never forgive you if you hadn't and if it did turn into something. I'm just thinking."

"Dogged if I didn't notice that."

"I don't know."

"Don't know what?"

"I just don't know what I'd advise anybody to do in a situation like that."

"Mebbe it's just possible that nobody'll ask you. Then you'll be all right."

"Oh, Wick," she murmured with impatience. "Let's go on up."

They turned out the lights and went upstairs.

XXXV

Eliza had the northwest corner bedroom, from which she could look out over the treetops toward the dome of the chapel. She awoke early and lay looking at the grey sky, the grey green of the oxidized copper dome, and the black claws of the topmost branches of the trees. She wished she did not have to get up at all that day. There was something she desired to think about all by herself. It was before her eyes, it was behind her eyes, and turn where she might, she was sure it would be in her sight until she spoke to it. For the first time in nearly four years she had a reminder, the smallest hint, of what happiness once was like; the first poor scarcely breathing presence of the idea that it might once again come to live where she was.

At a little past eight, there was a knock on her door. It was Vivi's maid, bringing a tray with coffee and orange juice.

"Mrs Grace thought you might want this before you went down to breakfast."

"Oh, I do. Thank you. Is everybody up?"

"Mrs Grace is dressing. Admiral and Mrs Thayer are downstairs with the Sunday papers."

"Thank you. I'll be down very soon."

The maid withdrew. In a moment there was another knock. It was Vivi.

"May I come in, Eliza?"

"Oh do, Aunt Vivi."

"I hope you slept well."

"Wonderfully. I was being frightfully lazy until your coffee tray arrived."

"I just wanted to tell you. Dorothy will arrive by car from Washington a little after nine. I have talked with the airport in Washington. We've sent the big car in to meet her, with Commander Morton, the aide. My car, of course. Avy does not use official cars privately. She will have time to freshen up a bit and then accompany us all to Chapel."

"I am dying to see her."

"I think she will be all right. The stimulus of arriving, and seeing people, and all that, will be good for her. It is of all the rest of the time that I cannot think without a heartache."

"I know."

"I had hoped you might have made some plans for her, Eliza."

"Plans?"

"After all, you are all that is left of her family. Her only link with David. I know she dearly loves you. If you could see—"

"I love her too, with all my heart, Aunt Vivi."

"If you could see," continued Vivi, riding through the interruption which nevertheless she kindly acknowledged with a

102

beautiful smile, "the things she has written me about you, during the trying times when you were both waiting together for the news that did finally come—"

Eliza nodded, her eyes wide open, and her face pale. Her heart began to beat like a little bird's. Her magnificent aunt was like a noble image of the law. She was grave, handsome and compassionate; her firm and musical voice spoke with the accents of duty; she was like an embodiment of majority opinion, and seemed as practically right and as inescapable. Eliza did not know why she felt so frightened. But she clasped her fingers under the covers and her thoughts began to erect clever defenses against she knew not what.

"Naturally Dorothy wanted to be with us all for a little while. We will do everything in the world for her. She will want to talk with Duncan. I daresay he has already brought you whatever details he could?"

"Yes."

"I can imagine."

Eliza shook her head, as if to say, No you can't. Nobody could.

"But of course," continued Vivi, "in due course, Dorothy will want to go back and resume her own life. It was for that that I hoped you might have had some intentions."

Eliza looked at her, and though she did not know it, or mean it to show, there was a proud smile in her face. She didn't speak. Vivi went on.

"And I think Dorothy is too—too selfless to mention anything at all of what is in her mind. But I am sure I know what it is. I only wonder if you do."

Oh yes, thought Eliza. I know. I think I know. I think it is probably why I did not want to get up this morning, but why I preferred to stay by myself and hold on for as long as I could to what else I knew, and wanted, and could not have for very long.

Vivi inquired of her with her splendid eyes as to why she did not answer?

"Perhaps I do know, Aunt Vivi," answered Eliza finally, in a soft voice.

"Then if you do, I know you well enough to have no worry. You are younger. You are stronger. You can be so great a help to her in every way. You both have difficult years ahead of you. You will need each other. Her house is big enough. You have helped in the shop before. We're all so delighted and proud of how well you have both built that up. Your friends will always be coming and going through Coronado. You know the life there already. I perfectly well realize that everybody must make her own decision. But I also felt that if you *knew,* you could only decide in one way. Am I right, Eliza, my darling? —I am only thinking of the happiness and companionship of my own sister and of yourself; we all feel you so truly to be of our family. We never want to lose you."

Without once uttering the word duty, Vivi had defined it, and had urged its meaning so truly upon her, that Eliza knew she must succumb to it. Whatever she said now was likely to be regarded in the light of a promise; a promise to the world, and, more binding, a promise to herself. There was every reason for Aunt Vivi to think as she did, and to say what she'd said; every reason, but one, and in all conscience, Eliza could not produce it now, for what it would mean in this household, where they were all gathered to observe—in a sense, to memorialize—David's death.

"Why, yes, Aunt Vivi—that is, if Doro really does expect me, and does look forward to—"

The answer to this was a profoundly compassionate smile, a confirmation that poured upon her from Vivi's blue-grey eyes, that were like star sapphires. She bent down and kissed Eliza on the forehead.

"I knew you would let nothing stand in the way of doing the finest thing in the world," she said. "I shall be downstairs. Come whenever you are ready."

She left the room.

With a feeling which if she could have translated it she would have expressed in the words, Oh, my poor new love, Eliza turned over and wept into her pillow. When she was able to recover herself, it was with a bitter hope that, since she had never really, flatly said to Duncan Richards that she was in love with him and wanted to marry him, he had not counted on it as much as she; and would therefore not feel so badly about how things were to be, from now on, for some years, anyhow.

xxxvi

If there was one thing Guinevere Grace had never been able to understand, it was how people could ever be late for engagements. To her, keeping an engagement on time was an inescapable condition of life, sometimes agreeable, sometimes not, like telling the truth; but always and simply necessary. She did not harshly judge those who were inclined to be late. Rather she seemed to regard them as victims of an affliction; less fortunate than herself. Some events could be delayed for late-comers, and when it was possible, smilingly she would wait. This morning, however, nothing could wait. Chapel would proceed on schedule.

She was waiting with her husband, the Thayers, and some casual friends of the Annapolis group, for Commander Morton to arrive with her sister. There must have been some delay at the airport in Washington. If they did not arrive in time she would ask someone to wait for them at the front door of the chapel with a message. And a message, too, for Miss Sarah Cleveland, that girl of Phil Morton's who was supposed to be here, but who also was tardy. Eliza had gone to Mass in Annapolis, and would join them at the quarters after Chapel.

It was a warm Sunday for January. Thinly overcast, the sun sent a silver light to earth. The winter grass was a dry golden green. The staff were already assembled, chatting with the Superintendent until they should all hear assembly sound in the formation area of Bancroft Hall. When it came, blown briskly, Admiral Grace stepped to his place on the right of the chapel doors with his staff ranged behind him. Admiral Thayer stood beside him as his guest. They were there to take the salutes as the chapel parade brought the Brigade of Midshipmen from their quarters to the Sunday morning service.

The band began to play. To sumptuous and lavish brass music, the columns of midshipmen began to move out along Stribling Walk, and make for the chapel. They marched strictly. The officers wore sword belts. All wore white gloves. Against the grey of the light, the walks, and the buildings, came the moving columns of dark blue uniforms, dark blue caps, and pale pink faces, like conquering forces. The beholder saw them come and knew that nothing could turn them back. They swung their white gloves, their shoulders moved gently but powerfully. By the harmony of their presence and their purpose, they seemed to create the music to which they marched. As each battalion commander appeared at the steps, he saluted and declared, "Good morning, Admiral." In return, he received a nod, a smile, a salute, and a greeting. When the heads of the columns were already entered into the chapel, the far ends of the columns were not yet visible. The moving streams of blue-uniformed young men flowed as if without end. Sternly they tramped their way to the altar, as if to make a truculent compact with the God of their fathers that He should hear their prayers, even as He could now hear their marching steps and look down upon the massed magnificence of their youth.

It was in the midst of this procession that Vivi heard voices and footsteps behind her as she stood watching the parade from her place by the euonymus bushes. She turned. It was Phil Morton, bringing Dorothy to her. She left her place and went to embrace her sister. They did not speak for a moment. Vivi could hear Phil explaining about a delay when Doro's plane had come down at the Tri-Cities airport in Virginia, and how they had hurried to be here in time for Chapel, and how they had barely had time to go to the Carlton in Washington for a cup of coffee and a brief freshener-up for Mrs Hopkinson.

Arm in arm, Vivi led Doro back to the walk to see the rest of the chapel parade. Once in place, she disengaged her arm, and placidly resumed her responsible review of the midshipmen as they passed. She was aware that, seeing these young men, her sister might also see David as he had marched to Chapel in other years. But she believed there was nothing in the world that could not be endured, and even transcended, if it had to be.

Diana Thayer embraced Doro with a word or two.

Commander Morton moved to take his place behind Admiral Grace. As he passed, Doro gave him a smiling nod of thanks for his kindness in meeting her, giving her breakfast, and bringing her here. She asked herself if it were so, and could hardly think so, but it seemed to her that as he silently acknowledged her little message, he blushed deeply.

Now she began to watch the faces of the midshipmen as they went by. They saw no one. Their expressions for the most part were severe. Over nothing, she knew. Simple severity was a canon of life, the garment of a soul unformed, a proper way to be, and it touched her because it implied an attitude toward life before they knew anything about living. She had seen it in David, and in his father, who in their times had marched here; and who in a certain sense, marched here still. Her head swam a little. Perhaps she had been foolish to come back here today, so soon, to see how they still looked as they strode in step so confidently to the brasses and the drums, on their way to the uncertainties with which they would, every one of them in his time, have to come to terms.

She was still very much like her sister in every aspect but coloring. She was dark and pale, where Vivi was blonde and rather high colored. Her dark eyes were shining. She was in black. There were shadowed hollows in her cheeks, though her face was not thin. Her cheeks were rather prominent, mostly

108

from the shape of a smile which she wore habitually when there was anybody around. Though she held her head high, she carried her shoulders a little raised, as if to shrink under, or fend away, a blow that might fall suddenly from an unknown source. Her whole bearing unconsciously confessed the events of the past few years in her life, and the terms with which she had come to meet them.

In another moment, the band music was ended, for the last of the midshipmen had marched into the chapel and the organ within began to pulse against the air with heavy tones. The little party on the chapel steps broke up.

Admiral Grace turned to Dorothy as she came up the steps, and kissed her. He said she looked splendid. She said she was a little tired. He denied that she looked it, and told her Eliza would meet them after Chapel. Vivi asked Commander Morton where Miss Cleveland was, as if he had invented her too cleverly out of whole cloth the night before. He said he had no idea. She knew perfectly well how to get here. Anyhow, they obviously couldn't wait. At a nod from Avy, they mobilized to enter the chapel, which was done with some ceremony, Avy going first with Vivi by his side, followed by Morton and Dorothy and the Thayers. As they entered, the regiment came to standing in the pews, the organ trumpeted and galed through a processional. The Graces proceeded to the front pew on the left where they were awaited by the midshipman brigade commander. When they were all well placed, the midshipman staff took places in the front right pew, and the whole congregation knelt for a moment, following the example of the Superintendent, his wife and their party, who on their knees, leaned forward, closed and covered their eyes, and made a communion with the presence and the occasion of that place. Then they sat back while the regimental choir arose, in their stalls flanking the altar which was deep in the sanctuary, and began to sing a hymn.

At the end of the hymn, everyone stood and waited.

Presently, casting a faintly multicolored shadow ahead on the floor of the aisle, there came, at a ceremonial pace, slowly and with a whisper of silks and fringes, a color guard with the flags of the United States and of the Naval Academy. The escort was armed with rifles. The guard passed up into the sanctuary, were received at the altar by the chaplain, and divided to place the American flag to the right, the regimental standard to the left, of the altar. The guard then reassembled and marched down and out of sight to the rear of the chapel.

This ceremony was accomplished in silence.

Dorothy Hopkinson had been here many times. She said to herself now that she must keep from regarding this as a sad occasion, or a melancholy place. And yet as in any place of many beginnings, confident, bold and high of heart in their times, there were sorrowful endings that could as justly be rooted here. Had sorrow properly any place in her thoughts this morning? Let her take her reality from the three thousand youths all about her in the chapel. The choir was nearing the refrain of the hymn. The air became charged with anticipation. In a moment it broke under the blast of the throng of young voices in the church which began to sing the refrain. They sang with their own deliberate pace, lagging behind the organist in spite of his strict efforts to sound the melody and accent the beat to keep them up to time. The result was a sort of casual splendor that lifted her heart, even as it flooded her thoughts with memories of her husband and her son.

These she must keep to herself. She knew that everyone was surrounding her with a climate of solicitude, and that comfort awaited her at the first sign of any need. Sitting in perfect poise, her head slightly lifted, her eyes roving over the faces of the choir as they sang, she said to herself that love when it had lost its object was tyrannical. If she indulged or encouraged it, it would become her master, not her equal. To fall down in grief before those memories that surged in her now would not only embarrass the family here; but would, she knew, create for herself another kind of trouble which she would be a long time undoing.

Her pulse was racing. The grandeur of the voices in the air pressed upon her. There was a youngster in the first row of the choir whom she could see in profile very distinctly. In a strike of recognition, she saw that he looked like David. He had the same curious earthen blend of color between his short golden hair and his rose golden skin. When he glanced down at his hymnal, the young man had shadows under his eyes like David's. His wide and finely shaped lips were smiling in the act of song, merely out of habit. Perhaps the likeness would vanish entirely if she ever saw his full face, in the kind of animation that might come over it in conversation. But now it was an idle resemblance which, coming here and at this moment, put a heavy burden upon her. She closed her eyes and begged the likeness to go away. When she looked again it was still there. In desperation her feeling rose, and she must thank God that there was such bounty in all of life that other Davids, the sons of other women, and the lovers of other girls, still walked upon the earth.

She must either praise life to the full extent of her suffering, or know the envy of the bereaved which had the impulse to destroy.

When the hymn ended, and there was a rustle of closing books, and the congregation arose as the chaplain came forward from his prie-dieu by the Academy flag, she leaned to Vivi next to her, and delivered herself of the blinding likeness by whispering,

"Do you see that third boy in the choir? Doesn't he look like David?"

Vivi raised her glass and gazed. She detected the resemblance. She nodded.

"Very much."

How like Dorothy that was. It was as if she had found a tactful and moving occasion to let everyone know that there must be no hesitancy about mentioning David, out of fear of her feelings. She turned to Doro with her head bent and smiled at her with her eyes. Doro felt the pouring look, but did not face to it. She merely smiled sidewise at Vivi, as if secretly, just as she had done years and years before, as a little girl, when she and her older sister had been leagued powerfully and ingeniously against the entire world, and possessed certain magic combinations and understandings which they were convinced had often worked wonders for them, which was true, as the powers against which they had invoked them were, however influential in their small lives, imaginary.

Now the chaplain was reading the lesson.

The regiment declaimed the responses with rise and fall of voices.

The chaplain called upon them to pray.

They all knelt.

Dorothy saw them cover their eyes with their hands, and bend their sunburned necks to the powers of the unknown. It moved her to see so much obedience from so much strength. She did not pray with them. She prayed for them. She felt that she must find and find again in herself such deeps of love from which to renew herself in life, or—or she would deserve to die. For it was her inarticulate but powerful belief that love was creative in any of its truly selfless terms, and fostered life, and was responsible for it.

Later on, this evening, tomorrow, she would ask to hear what she had come to hear. She wondered sometimes why she was at all interested in knowing any more about how David had met his end. Wasn't the fact by itself enough? Yes, she would think, perhaps it was. And yet, so strong was the tug of that communion and that embrace of another life which began with giving birth, she must know everything whether good or bad, happy or wretched, which that life ever knew. When he was a baby, and ill, the fever that was within him she fought from outside, cooling his strife with her hands and willing him to live. When he was a little boy and shamed by older playmates for feebleness and innocence in their childish imitations of worldly treacheries and evils, she mended his pride with the gift of patience. When he was a young boy, given to cynicism that hurt his parents for what it reflected upon their lives together, the condition of the world as they saw it and enacted it, she suffered him to hurt her if he pleased, for he was her son; and he had seen, and desisted. When he was a young man, married, rooted like a tree among his kind, she had known by the analogy of his own father's memory what strands needed weaving from how many other lives to make the strong knot that was a man's true heart. Why should she not need to know all that must be known about him as he died of this life?

Oh God, she prayed, that I may rise to meet it. . . .

There was a sermon, of which she did not hear very much, except that it was jovial, big-hearted, simple in its premise, and here and there studded with a joke, as a cake with a raisin, to engage the appetites of the young, and, further, to confirm them in the object of their presence here, which was to learn and to do their duty.

High up in the windows of the dome above them, the amber glass was turning to gold as the sun burned through the morning's overcast. The ivory colors of the chapel interior began to glow. A golden quality seemed to invade the scene, and when the organ next sounded, its tones seemed golden, like the very pipes from which they issued.

It was Hymn Number 415.

Dorothy remembered it in her bones. She knelt with all the rest of them and bowed her head. The choir stood and faced the altar. The organ gave out a brave trumpeting introduction. All the young voices in the chapel began with full power to address the noblest of all prayers in the Navy. As the hymn progressed, the regiment, by tradition and custom, sang each line more and more softly, until at the end, there was a huge sighing whisper of men's voices that was like the spirit of all the world's waters.

114

Eternal Father, strong to save,
Whose arm hath bound the restless wave,
Who biddst the mighty ocean deep
Its own appointed limits keep,
Oh, hear us when we cry to Thee,
For those in peril on the sea.

Amen

The familiar words, the grave and simple melody, and the earnestness of the young voices, made her shiver. The tears came to her eyes. They knew not for what they prayed, really. How beautiful were their voices. *Oh hear us,* they pleaded healthily until her heart turned over, *when we cry to Thee,* and yet it was a cry without feeling other than thoughtless content with well-being, appetite and the approach of the end of chapel, *For those in peril,* they chanted gently who had never known it, *on the sea, Amen.* Oh yes, Amen, she thought, meaning yes, oh yes, on behalf of any who might some day have her knowledge.

Now the ceremonial gravely reversed itself. The color guard came up the aisle again, marched into the sanctuary, took up the colors, and to a proclamatory wind of music from the organ, high pipes and grand rumble, came down from the altar and marched out of the chapel with all standing. The regiment followed, emptying the chapel by all the various doors, where they met girls who were waiting, and visiting families. When the church was all but empty, Admiral Grace arose at his aisle place in the front pew, stepped out, gave his arm to Vivi, and led his party down the aisle as the organ resounded in conclusion.

On the front steps, they found Eliza waiting for them. She came forward. She and Doro embraced. They exclaimed with the joyful sounds of a happy meeting. Each knew how the other felt, and also how everyone expected them to feel. They behaved as though nothing at all dwelt far down in their thoughts and obsessed them. Smiles everywhere. The sun was now shining. It was going to be a warm winter day. Visitors shook hands and chatted for a few minutes. The chaplain was complimented upon his sermon. A Sunday freedom was in the air. Midshipmen, out of ranks, were wandering along the walks in their own good time. Visiting girls were like winter flowers. Vivi looked upon the scene, and liked it, though she did not forget to look for Miss Cleveland.

"Well, I see she didn't come at all," she remarked to Commander Morton.

"No, she didn't. If I may, I'll go phone and see what's the matter. —I suppose she forgot to bring a hat. She never wears them."

Vivi nodded him away, and then led her party down the walk to the Quarters, where the halls were scented with new bouquets which she had finished arranging just before chapel. At the door, Avy took Doro's hand and in a little comedy of gallantry, conducted her over the threshold, and then put his arm around her and hugged her substantially. Then he stepped back, rubbed his palms together, and said there was something about it, he never could quite say exactly why, but there it was, just about this time before lunch every Sunday, he felt most powerfully thirsty.

xxxvii

Commander Morton called for Miss Cleveland at his own quarters. She was waiting for him in the book-lined living room. She wanted to know what it was going to be like. He told her it was a pleasant convention that after Chapel every Sunday, the Superintendent and his wife always had various friends in to say how do you do. Frequently there were visitors from Washington or Baltimore. Such guests were invariably invited to Chapel. In Mrs Grace's time, that invitation to Chapel was regarded very seriously.

"You'd think it was a command performance," remarked Miss Cleveland with asperity.

"Well, it is."

"But imagine!" murmured Miss Cleveland. "Do you mean I shall actually be expected to give an excuse for not being there this morning? I shall just simply say I overslept, in the first place, and in the second place, even if I had arisen with the lark, that it was most extremely likely that I'd have preferred to read the Sunday papers and wait for you to pick me up."

"I hope you won't, Sally," said Morton.

He couldn't convince her that this was a different world. She was, he supposed, conventional in her own way—knowing, intelligent and amusing. She'd grown up all over the world, and was lately returned from wartime duty overseas with the Red Cross. Her parents were dead. She had inherited money. She'd known Morton in New York. They had the same allusions, and until today had seen eye to eye about everything. She was tall and handsome, highly made up.

"I've already fixed it up with Mrs Grace," he said, modest over his cleverness. "I told her that you couldn't get to Chapel because you had not brought a hat. All you have to do is mutter something about that, and it'll all be over."

She was aghast.

"A most ingenious and tactful explanation, I am sure. I am such a bumpkin that when I go to spend a weekend, I neglect to arrive suitably wardrobed. Fat lot of chance my buying that. What do you call this, as a matter of fact?" She swept her gaze upward indicating the plumy hat that sat low upon her brow.

"I know. You'll just have to go without."

"!"

"Yes, I know, but you wouldn't want to make a fool of me, would you, Sarah? My position here is different. You'd never understand it. The Graces are wonderful. I'm nuts about all of them. But naturally, an aide—"

She gazed at him with a clinical air of speculation.

"So we compromise by making a fool of me. Well, as I do not belong to the USNR, I suppose that won't matter so much."

She took off her hat and laid it on the long low table where the Sunday pages of the New York Times attested to the agreeable morning she had spent.

As they walked over to the Superintendent's Quarters, she made him pay. In the lightest and most false of spirits she told Morton she *really did* understand his position, for she had been close enough to the war overseas to *realize* that officers frequently *had* to make all *kinds* of sacrifices and submit their *personal* convictions to the good of the *service*. In North Africa she'd became quite a *good friend* to a young major in the Field Artillery who held a *decided* personal conviction about *going on living,* and with *all* his members *intact,* preferably; nevertheless, one night, in a small unimportant action near El Gafsa, doing what he had to do, he had lost one leg and one eye, in a freak disposition of the shrapnel. So *naturally,* all this about absent chapel and missing hat was *easily grasped.*

They arrived to find the pre-luncheon party in full swing. All the people were out on the long sun porch. The voices rose in a clamor that was like the commerce of birds, heard from a distance. Everyone held a glass of one sort of another, or a cup of coffee. The white winter sunshine dazzled the thin white curtains along the solid glass front to the porch. Filipino boys in white coats were handing around trays of morsels. Vivi watched them, and everyone else, as it were with one eye, marshalling the whole party as necessary, even while she talked with guests. Now, though she was deep in a delighted conversation with Doro, Vivi saw the young woman with Commander Morton as they showed in the doorway. In a moment she would go to meet them. But not just yet.

The sisters had not seen each other for nearly a year. In any crowd, they had always been able to feel separate and intimate. It was as if, given any company at all, they still preferred one another's. Doro knew the generous sense of responsibility for others that lay under Vivi's grand ways. Vivi knew the kind of strength and spirit, even the high temper, that lay under Doro's grace of manner. Each had always felt a part of the other's history. They often disagreed. But they always in their thoughts allowed for that. It was part of their respect for each other. In the midst of the chatter, Vivi was talking seriously and tenderly to Doro.

"We want you here for as long as you will."

"I'll love it for a little while. —Then I'll have to go back."

"To the shop?"

"Yes."

"Alone?"

"I have taken on someone. I don't know how it will work out."

"That means it won't."

"It may, Vivi."

"My darling, you've always known about things like that the first instant. Well, I have some information for you."

"You have?"

"Eliza wants to go back with you and stay."

Doro put her head down and then looked up as if this simply could not be credited. Vivi saw her frightened pleasure at the idea, and her thoughts leaped up at the goodness in life.

"To stay?" said Doro. "Do you mean to come and live with me?"

"And yes: to work in the shop, as she did before when David first went out to the Islands."

"Did she tell you so?"

"Yes."

"When?"

"This morning."

"Oh, Vivi, what an impossibly marvellous thing for her to decide!"

"You had hoped," declared Vivi, nodding to confirm her analysis of each phase of Doro's feeling, "that she might want to. But you were of course reluctant to suggest it yourself. Yet it seemed to you the dearest possible solution to what you both really wanted. And it was of course David that you both thought of more than anything else."

Dorothy was almost a rosy pink and her eyes swam in pleasure. When the sisters were borne down upon by old Commodore Bixby (Retired), who as an almost professional widower had worn black crepe on his tweed sleeve for twenty-seven years, he stopped a little short in order to peer at Doro out of his ancient eyes, to make sure that she was as radiant as he had thought from a little distance.

"My eyes," he stated, "fool me up close. But I declare, Dorothy, you have never looked prettier. I always know the truth from across the room. It's what brought me over here."

Vivi left them.

She found Commander Morton and Miss Cleveland clustering with Cordelia Richards.

"Phil," she said, with an elevated sort of kindness, at the same time wondering why this tall, hatless, and handsome young woman with him had such fire in her eye, "I am sure this must be Miss Cleveland."

"It is," said Commander Morton.

"How do you do, my dear?" said Vivi. "Phil promised to bring you to see me."

"How do you do, Mrs Grace?"

Miss Cleveland suddenly thought she would be damned before she would make her excuses. That sort of feeling showed in her expression, however much she smiled. She reckoned without Vivi.

"We missed you at Chapel, my dear?"

It was kindly; but it was also expectant. Miss Cleveland felt she must be blushing a trifle, but she glanced at Phil who had turned away and was animatedly talking with the others. Oh, she thought, what difference did it make? If he really thought it important.

"Yes, I was frightfully sorry," said Miss Cleveland. "But the oddest thing. When time came to go to the services, I discovered I couldn't. I'd brought no hat."

Vivi smiled gently and shook her head a trifle.

"Any covering, my dear, would have done. A kerchief, or a scarf."

So much for Commander Morton's intelligent excuse. Really exasperated now, Miss Cleveland plunged on,

"Yes, but of course I thought the service here was so very formal, it would have been quite out of place to show up with just a—"

"My dear?" said Vivi, now in her most musical of tones, and with the most characterful of nods, "it is not costume that takes us there, it is worship. Have you met my husband?"

Avy was at hand, and he bowed humorously, like a boy at dancing school, till he looked like a figure seven.

"I know all about you, my aide has told me, and I have to keep in good with him, so come and have a cigarette with me, and tell me how to impress him."

Miss Cleveland was still gasping at what she viewed as a scolding. But Vivi went on her way, considering how really extraordinary it was that charming, handsome, obviously intelligent girls like Phil's Miss Cleveland grew up these days without a scrap of simple piety in them. She suddenly sighted Duncan Richards coming in, and he made her think of David, and of her own boys, who were safe somewhere at sea, and she took him in hand. She thought he looked better this morning. More at peace. Glancing around she saw Eliza by a window, doing a valiant job with two ancient ladies from Annapolis who lived on pensions and militant recollections of what they called the Fighting Fleet, meaning that so splendidly commanded at Santiago by Admiral Schley, on board the *Brooklyn,* as if the last American victory at sea had been that over Cervera, in which their long-dead husbands had figured.

"Liza, my dear," said Vivi, "give Duncan something to eat and drink. I want to talk with Mrs DeGroot and Mrs Cavanaugh."

Thoughtlessly, Vivi had invoked a discipline. Larger matters were already arranged, and it would of course be ridiculous to expect Eliza never again to face Duncan Richards.

The two young people moved away and leaned against the windows, looking down on the driveway court.

"Have you seen David's mother yet?" asked Eliza, looking up at him. Her eyes were like blue daisies, shadowed by a change of light.

"No. How is she?"

"She's wonderful."

"So are you."

"When are you going to have your talk with her?"

"When she asks me to."

"Yes. You must wait for that."

Pause.

"How much do you think I should go into it?" he asked.

"All the way."

"Really?"

She nodded.

"I wanted it," she murmured.

"I know."

"It may be one way to lay ghosts," she said.

His insides jumped at such a remark. It confessed so much, and seemed to know so much more than she possibly could know, such a girl, so pretty, so tired; but so full, this morning, of what seemed like mysterious purpose.

"D," she said.

"What?"

"I'm to go back with Doro when she goes."

"Well! That's fine. For how long?"

"To stay. For good."

"Well! I'm damned if I—"

"She really needs someone."

"Do you?"

"I don't know."

"Oh, Liza."

"I'm sure you see the point."

"Oh, hell, yes, I see the point!"

Across the room, Admiral Thayer saw the two of them by the glass, where the sunlight blurred all about their heads, golden and fiery. He knew what he knew, and warmly happy about them, and the party, and humanity in general, he came over to them.

They welcomed him, she called him Uncle Wick, a courtesy title, and Duncan excused himself, saying he must go and get something to drink for them all. But he didn't come back, and Wick suggested to his Honey Child that they mosey down the line to see what old Avy was up to.

The party was thinning out as lunch time approached. Nobody was particularly aware of it, but through sheer tactical skill, Vivi had disposed the forces of the gathering with appropriateness.

Commodore Bixby didn't know how it happened, but he found himself on the long couch with Mrs Cavanaugh and Mrs. DeGroot, and after the first shock of having lost the pretty wife of a lieutenant-commander a moment ago, he found that he and Mrs DeGroot and Mrs Cavanaugh had a good deal in common to talk about. Images of a long time ago began with a dim fiery relevance to arise in his mind. The old ladies thought Roderick Bixby was still one of the most fascinating men they'd ever known, and one of them—Mrs DeGroot—bridled believing that at one time she could have had him.

Cordelia Richards was telling Diana Thayer all about Duncan, and asking what to do about him.

As Wick and Eliza came by, she looked up and asked if anybody'd seen Duncan? Wick explained that the boy had gone to get them a drink and had never come back.

Avy was roaring at Sarah Cleveland who had just finished telling a story, at which she also laughed gaily. Commander Morton stood by her, modestly glad that she had made such a hit with the Adml, but nervously wishing she wouldn't laugh quite so hard herself. They all shifted unaccountably so that in a moment, Miss Cleveland and Eliza were face to face with Dorothy, and more or less by themselves.

"Didn't you come with Commander Morton? I'm Dorothy Hopkinson."

"Yes," replied Miss Cleveland. "Though I did arrive in disgrace. I am Sarah Cleveland."

"Why. Disgrace? What do you mean?"

"Our magnificent but formidable hostess," Miss Cleveland explained, "had invited me to Chapel, but I overslept and felt very lazy anyway. That fool Morton told me to say I'd forgotten to bring a hat. When I did so, Mrs Grace fixed me with the eye of a lioness and stated that I might have come anyway, in a scarf, or a handkerchief. When I pr-rotested," she said with exaggerated r's, "I was informed that here one went not for fashionable displays, but for worship. —I've never been so bruised in my life."

"Oh no," said Doro. "She didn't mean it that way at all."

"But you didn't hear it."

"No, but I know her. She is my sister, you see. She merely stated what is a fact, to her. She always states any fact."

"Oh my God," said Miss Cleveland, "what a miserable Sunday for me. I'm terribly sorry."

"No. Don't be. She would as openly expect you to state your position."

"If I did, she would now inform me that I had no business lying."

They all laughed. Eliza said, very much as Vivi might have, "But did you have?"

They laughed again.

"It is all Commander Morton's fault," said Sarah. "He's too nervous about it all."

The Navy wives smiled and shrugged at each other. How could anybody outside ever understand it, anyway?

There was another shift. Now Wick was party to Miss Cleveland, bending into her gaze, and tilting his head a little to attend her in the Natchez manner. It flattered her, for he was wholehearted about it. Eliza was left alone with her mother-in-law. Doro drew her a little farther down the porch, away from all the others.

"Liza, darling, what did you tell Vivi?"

"Oh. You know?"

"Vivi said—"

"Is it all right with you? Is it what you would like?"

"If you are sure."

"Oh, yes. Certainly. I've thought about it a lot."

"Well, darling, I'd have cut my tongue out first before I ever suggested anything of the sort. I would never want to be possessive about you. But you have brought it up, and you know I would rather have you with me at home and at the shop than anything in the world. It did work so wonderfully before, didn't it?"

"I always felt it did, Doro. —You are really happy about this, then?"

But she had only to look at Doro to know the answer to that. Her face radiated delight. There had been so few signs and moments of happiness there for so long, that Eliza was moved by the sight now to lean forward and kiss Doro on the cheek. As she did so, she shut her eyes and begged forgiveness of something within her for saying it no. But she had been brought to believe in the reality of self-sacrifice. There were larger considerations in the world than one's own self. This was like an *Amen* to her decision. She couldn't say it filled her with happiness. But perhaps that would come in time. Perhaps there were other values to discover first.

She excused herself with a little touch upon Doro's arm, and went to see if Aunt Vivi needed any help with the party.

But people were leaving, now, so steadily, that the party was reduced to the group still lingering around Uncle Avy. In a moment Vivi called him to come say goodbye to Commodore Bixby, who was going to drop Mrs DeGroot and Mrs Cavanaugh off on the way home. At the sound of that, the Commodore straightened up for a second and looked menacing and fierce, as seemed suitable to a squire of two dames. He glared first at one, then the other. His white mustache went awry at a dashing angle. The effort was brief, but impressive. Mrs De-Groot thought, "Mercy!" and Mrs Cavanaugh felt her heart beat a little more slowly, which was the way it always acted under excitement. Avy took them downstairs.

Doro was with the others, and asked Phil Morton if he hadn't better begin to catch her up on all the news. She had been gone so long. The family never remembered the very things she wanted to know.

Vivi overheard her, and laughed, as she came up, but said, "All right, Phil, go ahead."

"Well," said Morton to Doro, "one thing, I wish you had been here for—no, two things. The first was the launching of the great new carrier *San Jacinto.*"

"My ship," said Vivi, proudly, and smiled with warmth into the astonished eyes of Miss Cleveland.

"Yes, Mrs Grace christened her."

"Here is my bottle," said Vivi, taking a polished rosewood case from the table, and opening it. It contained a champagne bottle shaped of silver. On it was engraved the historical information pertinent to the occasion.

"The other thing," continued Morton, speaking to Doro, but they all listened closely, for suddenly he was impressive, "was

128

when I flew up to Brooklyn Navy Yard with the Adml, just before we went back out to the Pacific last June, when he decorated the survivors of the carrier *Jefferson*. That was a day I will never forget; and I will never forget how great, and I mean great, he was that day."

Avy was returning to the porch from the hall, when he heard these words. He stopped on the thick red carpet and then turned and tiptoed away, embarrassed to be hearing about himself. He went upstairs to steal five minutes with the radio in his bedroom. There was a newscast due.

Morton went on with his story.

xxxviii

On a morning in late June they had flown to New York from Washington in the Adml's plane. At La Guardia Field the big limousine with the 3-starred flag and the siren was waiting for the official party, with two other cars. It was a sunny morning. Everything twinkled in the light. They set off across traffic, the siren on the Adml's car growling and clearing the way.

At the Navy Yard they were received by the Commandant, the party was reshuffled among the cars, and they drove down the quayside streets, along which towered the mighty forms of war vessels, abuilding or under repair. Over the whole Yard hung a busy sound, as of a swarm of giant bees. Spouts of white steam from working engines spiralled into the summer blue sky. When the cavalcade rounded a corner, past a long red brick shop building, and came under the shadow of a rusty cliff with raw pine scaffolding and stairways built against it, there was not an immediate realization that this was a ship's hull, so huge it was and so battered. The cars rolled up to the middle stairway and stopped. Avy led them up the gangway. At its end they turned into a twilight of cavernous shadow, broken by a well of bright sunshine that came down from above.

They were in the hangar deck of the USS *Thomas Jefferson*. The piercing smell of dead fire was still in her. Her whole interior walls were a towering mass of wrenched and rusty steel: pipes, girders, stanchions. The flight deck which normally would have closed out the sky was entirely gone from the forward elevator aft. In this cold and tortured mold, the rage and fury of the ship's suffering and crippled survival were fixed and could still be read, as if in mammoth intaglio. How she could have floated at all, much less found her way home under her own power, it was impossible to imagine. Fire, explosion, and their multiple infernos, had not been able to sink her on that early morning off Japan when Japanese suicide planes had found her with her airplanes in the hangar deck loaded with rocket bombs, ready to be lifted up the flight deck for takeoff. What the visiting party thought of was what must have been suffered by the frail human bodies of this ship, if the steel strength of it showed this violence of destruction.

The Captain of the *Jefferson* led Avy and his party forward, where they came to a huge slope like a vast table top, lying awry, with its top edge hung on the flight deck a story above, and its bottom edge lying here on the floor of the hangar deck. It was the forward elevator, twisted and blown down into this grotesque position; so it had travelled all the way home. Up the

130

sharp flat slope wooden cleats had been hammered, and a handrail had been built. It was the only way to reach the remnant of the flight deck, the forward third of which was still in place. They climbed up and as they appeared, the Admiral's music was heard. A hollow square of seamen and a double row of officers standing ahead of them came to attention. A handful of visitors, newsreel cameramen and radio broadcast men were disposed near the bows of the ship. A light breeze off the harbor whipped freely about.

The Admiral and his party took their places facing the formation. There was a long silence on the forward flight deck as Avy looked them over. Below, and aft, and on the docksides, with not a pause, the work of repairing the giant cripple went on. Riveters hammered. They could hear the grind of machine shop lathes. In the sunlight an arc-welder far aft made a dazzle of brilliant blue and green blaze. Even in the bright day, the far end of the *Jefferson* seemed to diminish in a haze, like a perspective of city blocks far away.

These were the men who made the soul of the ship, and they stood here waiting. They had lost nearly a thousand of their fellows, in burn and crush, choke and drown. Their ears had heard such sounds. Their eyes had seen such furies. Their bodies had felt such fleeting chances. Their ship would have gone to steam and oblivion but for their grasp of life. Coming home, through storm across the Pacific, through the Canal, and up the coast, they had improvised their way. Arriving at last off Gravesend, they merely said they were glad to be back. When the pilot came up to board that still reeking wreck, he heard the crew singing like children returning from a tiring excursion into the country, "The old Tom-Jeff, She ain't what she used to be, Ain't what she used to be, Ain't what she used to be—" She was here today, at rest and as it seemed patient under the reconstruction that was being rushed so that she could be returned to service in the war.

Avy searched the last of their faces. Morton was standing beside him, holding the list of citations which he would read out when the time came. He hoped he would be able to make himself heard. Those were poor, thin and ridden faces, weathered, and with burning eyes, in the sunlight of this airy morning at home.

Avy had his speech all written down. He laid it on the lectern which held the microphones before him. The cameras began to turn. He glanced at the first page, and then did not need his text. He spoke only a few minutes. He said that in a moment or two, he was going to honor, on behalf of the people of the United States, those men here before him who by their exemplary conduct and courage had afforded their nation and their service yet another illustrious episode for history to perpetuate. Now, let him speak of those who had lost their lives. He reviewed the attack, the misty dawn, and the hours when it had seemed that the ship must perish. He had been himself in such action from the Coral Sea onward. He made them feel their common experience. And then he said that the strength of how America felt and lived lay in its recourse to what its people jointly desired to do; the way that will was carried out by the Nation as a whole; the way some were if need be ready to die for it; the way their dying for it made it more precious than ever; and the way no deaths in its behalf were lost or wasted if those who survived remained true to it. Here in this cold volcano of a ship was the racked but triumphant testimony to the glory of those who had died in her; for such a cause, which those who stood before him now must ever wear in pride and responsibility. He prayed God to preserve them all in that memory of their comrades.

He stepped back from the microphones and squared himself against his own emotion, and nodded to Morton, who came to the microphone, and began to read the citations as Avy moved out with the Captain of the *Jefferson* to decorate the men waiting for him there. Afterward they were shown over the whole of the ship, and had lunch in the Captain's cabin, and then flew back to Washington. But those who were there to hear Avy's words spoken over that battered and mending ship had a feeling of peace and resolve, which was expressed again by a number of letters from men of the *Jefferson's* crew who wrote to him, saying in their various ways that he had reached what they felt but could not say.

xxxix

Morton finished his recital of that occasion, and looked seriously into Dorothy's eyes. Everyone was reached by it, but only she really received his thought, which was proper, as it had been intended for her alone. What he meant it to say to her through this anecdote of the sailors and officers of the burned-out carrier, and the cost of her battle, was that he had her son David in mind, and wanted her to think of him, too, as he recalled aloud the healing words Avy had spoken of the dead that day. Her eyes blazed darkly in response. He saw that she was grateful.

They were all lost a moment in a little abstraction of feeling, almost of embarrassment. Then Doro said,

"Liza, where is Duncan?"

Liza knew that he had disappeared, and why. Nevertheless, she said, "I'll go see."

She went to phone the Richardses. Duncan answered irritably. He said certainly he knew he was invited to lunch, but now thought he would not come. Eliza must know how he felt. How could she expect him to hang around and be pleasant, under the circumstances? Would she please tell Mrs Grace for him? Eliza turned, for she saw her Aunt Vivi coming into the library.

"It's Duncan. He asks to be excused."

"Nonsense," said Vivi, taking the phone from her. "Lieutenant Richards?" she said with playful grandeur, "this is Mrs Avery Grace speaking from the Superintendent's Quarters. I do so want you to come to lunch, we have such interesting people on board, and I've promised them all they should meet you. You won't disappoint me?"

Eliza listened for the remote quack of his voice, but there was silence. Vivi glanced at her speculatively. Then he answered at last. He was laughing against his will. Vivi felt that her comedy had broken through one of his difficult moods, which had been caused by God only knew what.

"All right, thanks, Mrs Grace, I'll be there. —I don't have too far to go, after all," he added, with a poor but welcome attempt to match her comic convention.

134

Vivi hung up, and as she went out, though she said nothing, left Liza with the effect of a statement that that was how things like that should be handled.

xl

They went into lunch a little while later.

"Dorothy, my dear," said Vivi, who never used her sister's nickname, "you on Avy's right. Duncan, you between me and Dorothy. Wick, on my right. And Diana, you go to Avy's left, and Liza darling, in the middle."

They sat down. This left no one opposite Eliza, as they were an odd number, and it also had two women together, for Diana and Eliza were side by side.

"Liza lacks a man," commented Vivi, and was either too preoccupied or too disapproving to take notice of the sharp inward hiss that Duncan made at her statement. Lacked a man, indeed. What else did they think was killing him?

"Vivi, this is Sunday," said Admiral Grace at his end of the table, and bowed his head. They all copied him. He said, with his eyes squeezed shut and his head to one side, "Now hear Thy faithful call to Thee with thanks, dear Lord, for the bounty of this table, upon which, and upon these lives here present, Thy blessing we invoke through Jesus Christ our Lord. Amen. —Vivi," he added, awakening in high spirits from his dutiful little nap, "we must have champagne with this lunch. I feel speeches coming on."

She wished he would get the habit of thinking of such

matters a little ahead of time, but he had never done so, and she supposed after all that r.h.i.p., and she beckoned to the head steward, who leaned down to hear her instructions.

"Vivi," called Avy, "what became of Phil and that amusing tall girl of his? We should have kept them for lunch."

"As a matter of fact, I did ask them. But they couldn't remain. Old Mrs Morton was having some people in for luncheon. They had to return for it. —Besides, I think we do better here just as family, today. Don't you?"

It was a general question.

"We're glad to be included," said Diana Thayer.

Dorothy gave her a look of reference to their mutual past.

"I must say," said Eliza, "that Miss Cleveland is one of the most knowing females I have ever met. —Aunt Vivi, she thinks you're a lady dragon."

"Why on earth?"

"You evidently scolded her about missing Chapel."

"Scold I did not. I pointed out as kindly as I knew how that she mustn't feel shy about behaving perfectly naturally here, and that if she had sat on her hat and ruined it, I said, or forgotten it, I said, or anyway had none to wear, then just because it might *feel* odd to put a handkerchief on her head to come to the services, I said, she must understand that most of us would never have noticed a thing, I said, for it was the worship for which we attended Chapel, not a fashion parade. And that the opinion of anyone who might be critical, I said, about putting a handkerchief on your head in order not to miss divine service was not worth taking notice of in any case. I can't think what else I might have said that frightened her."

"I'd hardly describe her as being 'frightened,'" said Dorothy. "She seemed more indignant than otherwise."

"Then in time she will realize how foolish such an attitude is. I really began to live when I decided never again to be indignant, about anything."

Avy turned to Diana at his left.

"She honestly believes," he murmured in a hoarse whisper so they must all hear him, "that she is never indignant, about anything. I suppose this scar is a witness to her sheer kindliness."

He tapped his left temple, where a white scar showed through his short clipped white hair. All of them but Duncan knew he'd got it in a crash landing years before. Dorothy put her hand on Duncan's arm and said,

"He's a frightful liar. A *dreadful* liar. You mustn't ever believe a word he says. I love him very much."

Duncan blushed with amazed fondness for her. She seemed to love everybody, everything, in life. He had such sick deeps of loathing in him directed against he knew not what that he wished he could close his eyes and will some of her peacefulness into himself. He had never felt such generosity as he saw in her. He couldn't imagine why she felt that way; not with what she had been through. He winced when he remembered that soon he was going to have to tell her things that were appalling to hear. He took refuge in the past, and he remembered a golden evening.

"Do you remember, Mrs Hopkinson, when was the last time we sat together at dinner?"

"Certainly I remember. It was when you and David graduated. You gave a dinner party."

The whole lunch table listened to her, though she continued to speak to him only.

"I sat at your right, and I think David sat at the other end. Or was it Eliza?"

"It was me," said Eliza, like a little girl. "It was both of us."

"So it was. —I even remember what we talked about."

"You do!"

Duncan turned whiter, if that was possible. He was about to pursue the subject desperately, when Avy spoke.

"I have always had an unworthy suspicion that there were some shenanigans going on at that party. I know all us grownups had cocktails, and the young sprouts all stood around drinking tomato juice with virtuous grins on their faces. But I wouldn't fall down dead with astonishment if I were now told that various phone calls, and messages, and calls of nature, et cetera, which took some of the handsome young gentlemen away for a moment or two at a time, had to do with fortifying their general gaiety."

Wick Thayer called across to Duncan.

"How gracefully do you think that comes from one who in his day discovered the exhilarating properties of lemon extract, and shared the discovery with his classmates?"

The lunch was being served all this while. The silver champagne buckets had been brought in and established on the sideboard.

"Back to the islands for you, after that," said Avy to Wick.

"If I could have the same plane I came home in, it would be a pleasure, Avy. —I had a MacArthur seat, and slept most luxuriously all the way."

"Sir?" asked Duncan a little stridently. "What kind of a seat?"

"I said a MacArthur seat. Meaning one of unusual comfort, as distinguished from ordinary plush, not to speak of buckets."

"Oh, I see," said the young man. His red hair was cut so short that it was in a perpetual bristle. Now it seemed to express him truly. "My naval unit served directly under General MacArthur. I always prick up my ears when I hear his name. He is a great man."

Duncan looked straight into Eliza's eyes as he finished his truculent statement. He seemed to be calling to her with all such misspent emotion. She pursed her lips and begged him silently not to trouble her further about what was already so difficult to bear. There was an unspoken conspiracy to divert the awkwardness created by Lt. (j.g.) Richards.

Admiral Thayer leaned to Vivi and said he had never tasted such a wonderful creamed shrimp. Admiral Grace took up his champagne glass and arose.

"Ladies and gentlemen, the President."

They all stood and drank it with him, and sat down.

Dorothy said what a curious thing it was; every time she heard that word, or saw it in print, she had to pause a moment and adjust her mind to it, before she was perfectly sure to whom it referred, for the first one that came to mind every time was the *late* President. Diana replied that she had the very same trouble, if you could call it trouble, not that that was what she meant.

"I always remember him," said Dorothy, "as he was that day at Pensacola, when Avy had him up to the Quarters for a little talk and a rest on the porch, and I was visiting you there after

Hoppy died. It was a very hot day and the juleps were very tall and simply snowy all on the outside. Until I saw him that day I never had any idea of how crippled he was. They had to help him every step and lift him and set him down and take him up. And yet he went everywhere, he did everything, he flew all over the world to fight the war, and he knew there was nothing impossible if you believed in anything enough. I have never been able to understand what was behind the cruel things people liked to say about him. After I was presented to him that day I had a great many new thoughts. I think they made me rather ashamed of myself. I think I had been feeling very sorry for myself. I have a bad temper, you know."

"Nonsense," said Wick gallantly.

"Oh, no, it's perfectly true," said Vivi, beaming serenely upon Dorothy. "That's what makes her so wonderful. She never loses it."

"Anyway," resumed Dorothy, "I went upstairs to my room, where I could still hear the humming of talk on the porch, with Avy, and the staff, and the President and his people; and I asked myself how long I expected to go around feeling so numb; and whether there might not be a somewhat different course to set myself. So I sat right down and wrote down a heading for a list."

"What did it say?" asked Duncan with veiled bitterness, as if he would gladly profit by her experience, but did not expect to.

"It said, 'The Future.' And I sat and thought for quite a while, and wrote down all the things I knew I could do if I had to. The last thing on the list was the thing I most wanted to do, but was most frightened of, because it had some book-keeping connected with it, and I cannot add or subtract, though I can multiply, even fractions, very well. I have never understood why. But the last thing was the word 'bookshop,' and it does not seem so very important to anybody else, but I thought about it and thought about it, and finally asked Vivi what she thought. And there you are. —I wanted to call it the *Recuerdos del Presidente a Pensacola Bookshop,* as they would in Mexico. Anyhow, that's how I always thought of it."

"And now you can add and subtract, too, can't you?" said Diana. She turned to the rest of them with a droll smile. "I taught her to. We got a little arithmetic book, Wentworth and Smith, and I corrected her papers in the evenings."

"David used to love the Mexican store signs so," said Eliza. "He taught me to remember several. I remember one, a shop in Mexico City, he used to talk about, called *Recuerdos del Porvenir.*"

"What does that mean?" darkly inquired Duncan.

" 'Memories of the Future,' " she said.

"That is my theme song," he said to her, grimly.

Vivi asked herself what was the matter with him. She decided the only thing to do was consistently miss his point, so long as he felt so disagreeable.

"It cannot really mean anything to you," she declared, kindly. "I remember all about the shop, myself. It was named *after* a shop called *El Porvenir—The Future*—which had burned down. So the good man built a new one, and named it, in a burst of sentiment, in memory of his first one. *Memories of the Future.* —In a sense, we all do that, with our lives."

Dorothy and Vivi held one another's eyes. They had one of

their moments of deep, personal, exclusive communion such as often overtook them in the presence of others.

"We make, or we imagine, something," continued Vivi with a glistening look for her sister, "and life comes along and destroys it, or changes it. And then we take what may be left, and we use it to build on, and imagine with. Don't we?"

"We always have," said Dorothy. Then with an effect of returning to the others, she smiled across at Wick.

"There was also an establishment," said Wick, "which I remember from our time in Chile. Its purpose will be explained by its title: *Las Delicias de Margarita.* —I hasten to add that I was never in the place."

Laughter from the two admirals.

"We used to come home and write them down," said Dorothy. "Hoppy adored the Mexicans. We gave a copy of our list to the Ambassador."

"You did love Mexico, didn't you?" stated Vivi.

"We adored it. Almost best of all."

"You remember, Avy," said Vivi, "we thought we were going to Mexico, the year that Papá died?"

"That was one of your years in Washington, wasn't it?" asked Wick.

"Yes. And I must add that we were very gay, in a suitable manner."

Duncan looked around at the faces of the older people. How much they shared. How contented they were with their histories. Their allusions appeared to be grateful and complete. Had they never lived, any of them? Perhaps they simply had no capacity to feel. Without a doubt none of them had ever gone through what he was going through right now. He supposed if they had any inkling of it, they would be mature and arch about it, and refer kindly to "a disappointment in love," as if there were a sort of norm by which such a situation could be measured, classified and dismissed. He thought that even Eliza belonged to their party. Today just to look at her made him lump his jaws. She had her pale blonde hair parted in the middle and brushed back straight over her ears and tied with a piece of black ribbon around which she had twined some artificial pearls. She sat facing the windows. Her blue eyes were sky blue. Her face was pale and he thought a little thin. Her mouth was brightly rouged but it didn't look shiny or sticky. He couldn't help staring at it.

"That was the year we all got so worried over Avy and his opera singer," said Diana.

The two young people turned on their host with astonishment, and then self-forgetful for a moment stared at each other.

"She was a very beautiful woman," said Dorothy, lightly, but with the air of one who would explain to the world so many years afterward what could have caused emotion now long vanished.

"I shall never live it down, that much is clear," said Avy, flushed with this family legend and its unspoken comic references to danger and prowess.

"What on earth is all this, Aunt Vivi?"

"My dear! You have heard of the prima donna, Lily Remusat. That winter we were speaking of, she gave a grand concert in Washington. We all went, naturally. Avy and I and Diana here, and one or two others, sat in a box near the stage.

My husband has always been a striking and handsome figure. Madame Remusat—"

"I wish," interrupted Avy, "I'd always known that."

"—Madame Remusat," repeated Vivi raising her voice over the interruption and speaking a little more slowly, "spotted him and, as she was famous for her emotional extravagances, she directed the whole of a very amorous aria at him, to the delight of the audience. We were transfixed. Your uncle blushed a deep crimson—"

"Never."

"—deep crimson, and threatened to leave the hall."

"What was the song?"

The Admiral astonished them all by stating the answer.

"A piece called 'Depuis le jour,' from the opera 'Louise,' by Gustave Charpentier."

They stared at him. He smiled privately and modestly.

"You don't mean Georges Carpentier, do you, by any chance?" said Wick.

Vivi answered.

"No, he's right, perhaps he is a little suspiciously right. —But that isn't all. We went to the White House afterward to a reception, where none other than Madame Remusat was to sing again. And there she and Avy were introduced. I must say I thought her behavior was comic in the extreme, even while it revolted me, and everyone else there."

"Except Avy," said Diana, with privileged malice.

"Except Avy," agreed Vivi.

Eliza said,

"But my dear Uncle Avy, I never knew this wonderful story! What happened next?"

He waggled his head from side to side very slightly, and pursed his lips as if to speak, but with much whimsical light dancing in his eyes, he hesitated, as though framing his answer very carefully. Before he could deliver it,

"Nothing happened next," interposed Vivi coolly. "Remusat returned to New York to sing at the opera. And I will concede that she was a magnificent looking woman, and that she made a great career for herself out of most unfortunate beginnings."

Avy gave up planning any further answer. But Wick thought he had a look on his face which could mean that he knew what he knew.

"Well," said Eliza, "where is she now?"

"She lives in retirement at Santa Barbara," said Dorothy. "I saw her there a year or two ago."

"And how does she look?"

"Comme ça." Dorothy made a gesture that outlined great obesity. —"With a face like a Hallowe'en pumpkin much rouged and powdered."

Avy came out of a smiling abstraction.

"That's nothing," he said, referring to the whole episode. "I have a signed photograph of Sarah Bernhardt upstairs in my study. Signed with my name on it. I went backstage as a midshipman. I offered to show it to Miss Cleveland."

"We have all seen it, darling," said his wife.

"It is a wonderful thing," said Dorothy, "but sometimes something you heard in music, or saw in a book, or a painting, a long time ago stays alive and seems to mean more every time you think of it. I remember in that winter of the war when I stayed in New York, and Hoppy was on convoy duty, and coming into town every few weeks or so, and we had such wonderful times, I suppose because they were so short and we had to pack so much into each one, one night he took me to the opera. We dressed ourselves up to the nines. Of course he was in uniform, but he carried white gloves, and he had just added his next stripe, and I called him Commander five times a minute. He made me wear a very low dress, and paint more than I liked to, and he ordered a fabulous corsage, white roses to go with my white satin dress and white satin slippers. I had my diamond bow knot in my hair. He liked to see me wear long white gloves, because he said he liked to take them off when the time came. . . . It was snowing. Hoppy said it snowed to match my costume, and that it was only one of the things that were going to insure a perfect evening. Anyway, we had wonderful seats in the second row, and I felt perfectly sure we were stared at all evening because we were so handsome, the pair of us."

Lieutenant (j.g.) Richards was sure it had been true.

"The opera was 'Tosca' and Geraldine Farrar was singing. When she walked on the stage in the first act, Hoppy grasped my arm so tightly that it hurt. He leaned down and whispered that she was the most beautiful thing he ever saw. And she was. Her voice, her acting, her face, and all the things that happened in the rather wild story, and of course all the music, put us in raptures. And the applause was wild. They called her back time after time between the acts. In the second act she wore a diamond tiara, and Hoppy said there were simply no two ways about it, he would simply have to get me one. He thought they did a lot for a woman. And I had felt so glamorous in my diamond bow knot! We went out and drank champagne between the acts after the curtain calls were all over each time. He kept exclaiming that it was a wonderful love story. Everything in the music, even, was about love, he said. Just as if he had made an exciting discovery. We both suffered terribly through the gory last act, so tragic, the things that happened to the lovers. When it was over, the house went mad when Farrar came out alone, and Hoppy turned to me, and said Do you mind, and he took away my white roses and he stood up and threw them to the stage. She saw them come, and where they came from, and she took them up, and because he was a naval officer in uniform, and so handsome, and we were at war, and everything, she took a step forward, and indicated him with the roses, and bowed deeply to him. The house watched and turned to see him, and applauded louder than ever when they saw who it was, a naval officer, and he did look splendid, and he took up my hand, and he bowed back to her on the stage, and then without taking his eyes off her, he took my hand, and kissed it, as if it was hers. I know she understood what he meant, because she smiled a dazzling smile and raised her shoulders as if he were kissing her hand when he kissed mine, and then she stepped back, and the curtains rushed together. —Somehow it has always stayed bright and vivid to me. The grand manner, for one thing. So much red velvet. So many gold lights."

They savored it in silence for a moment. Duncan who had spent much time in the hospital reading modern psychology sternly wondered, even though his heart ached for her, how she could tell a story like that and never for a moment glimpse its up-to-date implications, which obviously had to do with the secondary transferral of an emotional adhesion, through a clearly recognizable flight impulse, to a substitute image of the emotional desideratum, who happened in this case to have been a famous opera singer. Such clinical qualms troubled no one else.

"He really did have a feeling about music, didn't he?" said Vivi. "I remember in Boston, you were always going off with him to Symphony Hall."

Dorothy laughed.

"I think it was then more a feeling about me, than music. I think he always had to have the *combination,* in some form or other." She laughed again, and the rest of them felt like joining her. "I took him to Mrs Jack Gardner's to a musical, and there was a female 'cellist who nearly drove him mad, she was so homely, and yet she played divinely."

"It's a most unsuitable instrument for ladies, I always thought," said Vivi.

"Just the opposite," murmured Wick. "Spreads their legs."

"What was that?"

"Nothing. I just thought of something."

"You are a very bad boy, Admiral Thayer."

"Almost as bad as that Seward Hopkinson that time in Peking," said Dorothy. "Do you remember?"

She glanced around the table. But there was nobody there who had been in Peking when she was.

"He was no relation," she added, for Duncan's benefit. "Only the same name, but the odd thing was that he lived in the same apartment house as we did. One night someone brought him home very late and very tight, he was a bachelor, and dumped him in our door. Hoppy was up the river on a mission for a few weeks. Nobody at home but young David and me. Nobody ever discovered how our door had been unlocked. Anyway, Mr *Seward* Hopkinson spent the night in my drawing room with his head under my red lacquered chow bench. There was a lady waiting impatiently upstairs for him all that time. When my *amah* arrived the next morning early, she found him and woke him up. He was simply terrified of where he was. He thought he had gone mad. But the *amah* helped him. She led him to a window and pointed out where he was, and then took him to the hall, where he saw our name on the card above the bell-push. He went on upstairs with a terrible headache. That afternoon he came back down to pay a formal call and apologize. He even told me about the offended lady, who had got it out of him where he'd spent the night. He said he told her thoughtlessly, but he knew my reputation would not suffer. I told him he was ever so naïve if he thought Peking left anybody a shred of any kind. His lady friend certainly did her best with mine later. So he felt very guilty and claimed that if I did not forgive him he would drink himself to death. I promised him that he was well started without my presence in the case. He got to be a frightful nuisance, though he was a very amusing man, and very successful and clever. He made the most violent love to me, and brought David all sorts of presents, and even said he was dying to know my husband. I think he saw himself fitting very comfortably into an arrangement."

She paused for a bite.

"Then what?" asked Wick.

"Then Hoppy came home, and you know Hoppy. Somehow, we never saw much of Mr Seward Hopkinson after that."

It was a formless little story, but it interested them all, for it was about one of them, and it had the fringe of scandal in it as gossip, and that was always part of their worldly interest in what went on.

To Duncan Richards it was, though, a great deal more. He turned squarely upon his chair to gaze at her. He was suddenly alive to her as a person, in an entirely new way. She seemed his contemporary now, or he seemed hers. She had been pursued by love, she had known what it was all about. She could sit here and talk about it. It wasn't, with her, just a matter of highly decorated sentimental memories. She had a clear little vein of comic realism. He could visualize Mr Seward Hopkinson and speculate upon his plight. His heart gave a leap. Maybe she would get his point, if there were any way in the world for him to make it to her. Then he thought, Oh God, I am tired, and slumped down again in his chair staring at his own thoughts.

"The most ridiculous thing happened to us," said Eliza, "on *our* honeymoon." The family manner was in the air, like a ball to be tossed from player to player. It was her turn. "We were staying a few days at Lake Winnipesaukee, in a hotel near a place called The Wiers. We loved it all, being alone, and fooling around all day, taking little drives, and so on. We didn't even mind it when people would make references about bride and groom. But we got singled out once too often. Another honeymoon couple turned up, and we saw them watching us and we knew they were talking about us. We didn't especially want to meet them, but one evening the other groom came over to Davie on the porch just after sunset. It was a marvellous evening, the lake was beautiful. There was always a red light reflected way across the lake that we could never decide about. I insisted that it was the very reflection of Mars which was low in the sky, and very bright; but David said nonsense, it was just a little red light on a moored motorboat. Anyway. This fellow introduced himself and said he and his wife had just been married, and they knew perfectly well *we* had just been married, and in the most civil way on earth, he came over to inquire if we both would like to get drunk with them a little later that evening."

She stopped, and with her eyes wide open, treated them all to her china blue gaze.

"And did you?" demanded Duncan.

"Maybe we did," she replied. "I honestly don't remember. But I know the idea fascinated me, of *setting out to get drunk*. Not just have it happen because you were having a good time, and so forth and so on. But go do it as an end in itself. I found out something new every day."

Everybody, remembering that she was talking about her bridal days, burst into laughter at that, and had the satisfaction, in which they felt compassionate, of seeing her blush deeply at her own innocent remark.

Duncan was inwardly writhen at the story. It proposed to his imagination such lost intimacies that he could hardly bear to think of them. He saw her then as she must have been with David. He saw David as that strongly made and comely man with a youth's character. And then he saw him as he had left him in his grave, and he ground his teeth with his lips pressed shut.

There was an exchange of a gleam between Avy and Vivi. Suddenly, by common consent, there fell a silence, during which Avy arose, putting his hands into his coat pockets, with his thumbs showing. They all looked at him, and then with a heartbeat of premonition, Dorothy looked away from him, and down.

"My dear old friend and esteemed colleague, Admiral Thayer here," he said, rather formally, but with his voice lighted by emotion, "once remarked that we had some 'pretty considerable fellows in this war.'" He paused and looked at them all as if to gain their power in aid of what struggled to be said. A look of stern sadness went over his face; and then he smiled rather seriously and went on. "I think he spoke truly. I have served under, and I have held command over, some of the best and also simplest men God ever created, from the topmost rank to the most unrated sailor and I have seen them in some pretty bad situations. I have seen our whole country in a situation much worse at one time than most people realized or ever admitted to themselves. And I have watched our forces perform prodigy after prodigy, through what toil and suffering can never be related, in order that people can gather here today, free and safe, in my own dining room, and at my own table, and in every other dining room and at every other table in the United States. To bring us to this happy condition, which stands for so much, our country made out of the general run of our usual everyday living, a generation of heroes."

He looked at Diana Thayer, and she looked up at him. There was written on her face what he was leading up to.

"That is a shopworn word, until a time comes that gives meaning back to it. We have lived through such a time. But no man is a hero all by himself, just because he is called upon to be. There is always someone and something behind him that gives him what he needs. As I can name you those men who deserve our prayers and our thankful memories, so I can name

152

you those two women who have been the honor of our family in all the saddest experiences of hope and of loss, in the war lately ended. My wife and my friends kept me informed throughout the months and years how these heroic women in our own family faced their silent battle day after day, until that day when news came which made it seem as if they had lost it. Now, I will simply testify that how they met the assaults upon their fortitude, and how they honored the sacrifice of the son and the husband whom they lost, was an endless source of strength and conviction to me, and to all the many others of my comrades who knew, as I knew, the story of that lonely battle which went on at home, in so many homes, until after the surrender."

He paused again, and with his right hand lightly quivering touched the three silver spoons beside his plate.

"Well, you all know with me that that battle was not lost; though of course, like any battle, it could have been. I will have recourse at this point to some words of William Shakespeare's which I have thought over very often when I found out that these particular members of our family were going to assemble here today, for the first time since the end of the fighting. 'The peace of heaven is theirs who lift their swords in such a just and charitable war.' I don't think it would be seemly for me to offer comfort. What have I to say to her who can tell me what grief is like? But I can give my love, and my respect, and I ask you to rise and drink with me to our beloved Doro, and to our dear Eliza."

After lunch they moved lingeringly into the small green Brazil room to have their coffee. Mrs Grace took Diana Thayer's arm and drew her a trifle away from the others.

"I must tell you, Diana."

"What is it?"

"It couldn't be more of a relief. I was really quite terrified of what today might bring. But this morning, when I had made the barest mention of our darling Dorothy's future, Liza settled the whole thing for us all, and in the happiest possible fashion."

"What did she do?"

The two women exchanged a long and direct look, golden-lighted from Vivi, and crystal black from Diana. They were the oldest of friends. They had few secrets from one another, perhaps because each knew the other could not dissemble successfully for very long against the habit and astuteness of the other. Yet just for a moment there was the smallest hesitation in Vivi, as if in exchange for this information, there should be a compensation forthcoming from Diana, perhaps a nugget of gossip, or shop-talk, or a new facet of someone's character, which might prove to be a small unit of power in that womanly world of society which was fueled by what someone said to, or about, someone else. Their locked glances broke apart when Vivi smiled with the air of a victor too gracious to press an advantage, and said,

"Eliza has decided, and this morning told me so, that she is going to return to Coronado to live with Dorothy, help her to run the bookshop, maintain her little house, keep her mind off herself, and in general, help her—as they will help each other —to weather the very difficult next years."

"How extraordinary!"

"What is extraordinary about it?"

"Perhaps I do not quite mean extraordinary. Perhaps I mean how unexpected!"

Vivi smiled at the wall, as if in the kindness of a wisdom which is content to wait.

Through Diana's head raced all the thoughts that had been lodged there last night, when Wick spoke of the Richards boy and his hopes.

"Does Doro know?" asked Diana.

"Of course," said Vivi, with a warning glance, so that the others who were drawing near would not imagine that they were being talked about. "I told her this morning after Chapel, and Eliza spoke to her too."

"Of course she is delighted."

"I nearly cried to see how happy it made her. Here are the others."

It was after three o'clock when the coffee tray was taken out. Conversation was idle and easy. Vivi remarked that Diana hadn't said much since lunch. She replied that she had a small headache, and when Wick went up for his nap, she believed she would go too. It was a sort of Sunday afternoon signal. Admiral Grace always took forty winks after lunch on that day, with the Sunday papers at which he would now have his first chance. Some days, he said, he read straight through, and others he would doze off, occasionally awakening to find himself under a sort of tent consisting of the sports section.

"Some people are coming in to tea after five," said Vivi. "Wouldn't you like to come back then, Duncan?"

He gave Dorothy a troubled look with a frown. What did she want of him?

Before Dorothy could answer him, she must speak to her sister.

"Do you want me to help you with tea, Vivi?"

Mrs Grace leaned forward fingering her chain.

"If you would, I am more or less counting on you. If you should feel tired, you could slip away after a bit. But it would be nice if you could start us off."

"Then I'd love to."

Dorothy looked at Duncan. He scowled now. He thought she looked so tired, so ridden by the energy of her courage and her poise that he could hardly imagine her going through one more party today. But she smiled, and looked down, and then looked up at him again, in the little habit she had, and he knew that whatever she agreed to do, she had the power to fulfill.

"Would you come back to tea, Duncan?" asked Dorothy.

He swallowed. He believed that she wanted something of him. He stared at her, and said,

"Certainly."

Vivi with a cool and serene smile took his agreement to herself, as was proper, though he might not recognize it, and said,

"That will be divine. Now why don't you and Liza go for a little drive?"

They all looked at Eliza. She thought they looked at her like

156

a battery of searchlights. She could feel her color rising. She said she would very much like to take a little drive, and take some air, and see the country in its winter colors. It was a warm afternoon. There were so many places she used to know which it would be pleasant to see again.

Going upstairs, Diana said to her husband,

"Come right along to our room, don't stop and fool around with Avy. I must ask you something."

He did not answer. It was not the sort of thing women said which needed an answer. But he grinned at the energy of it, and wondered what was on fire in her mind now. She was frowning and toothing her lower lip, and when they reached the upper floor, her steps could hardly have been shorter, brisker or more purposeful. She opened their bedroom door, stepped aside for him, and closed it after him.

"Diny, honey, you act just like a bride. You get me all excited."

"Don't be a fool, darling. Sit down. What did that Richards boy tell you last night?"

"I told you. He wants to marry Eliza."

"That *is* what you said, isn't it?"

"Why, certainly!"

"And you said that he had proposed to Eliza, didn't you, and that she had accepted him, but wasn't saying anything about it for the present, didn't you?"

He shut his eyes a moment and slowly wagged his head back and forth in humorous despair.

"Now wait a second, hon. I never went into any such detail as all that. I said—"

"But it is what you understood, anyhow, isn't it?"

"Yeh, well, maybe. Young Richards said he was in love with her and wanted to marry her."

"*Yes!*"

"And I asked him how does she feel about it, and he said—" He paused as if to think, but really to devil her, and she knew it.

"Yes! Wick! Go *on!*"

"He said that as far as he could tell, she felt pretty much his way."

"Is that all?"

"B'lieve it is, except mebbe—"

"Oh, *Wick!*"

"I'm just trying to remember actually. He did say he hadn't said anything to anybody else yet about it, except Eliza, of course. But he said even so, he had not spoken to her *straight out* about it."

She turned away from him in a gust of exasperation.

"Then what did all that mean that you told me last night?"

"Just what I said. I said to him, I asked him, did he have a feeling Liza knew? And he said, these are the very words, he said, 'Oh, she knows.' Very positively. I'm no actor, Diny. I can't imitate him for you. That's just what he said. But I didn't have any doubt in my mind when I left him, and when I talked to you, nor do I now."

She sat down in a white covered armchair and lighted a cigarette.

"Well, for heaven's sake, then, it's just as I said when we got in here a moment ago."

He shut his eyes and let his head back in comfort on the back of his chair.

158

"I give up," he said with his eyes shut and smiling, "if you can't see the difference between what I told you and what *you told me* I told you." He awoke. "Why, anyway," he asked, "what's all this about?"

She told him what Vivi had said to her after lunch.

"'If Doro knew it, it might break her heart."

"It might," said Wick. "Let's not anybody tell her."

Diana's eyes were dark with thought. She smoked deeply on her cigarette. She was speculating in some distance from which he was exiled.

"And yet," she murmured, "I would bet my hat she would want to know it."

"Now, Diny."

And yet he too began to wonder on what terms Dorothy would like to assure her future companionship, and whether Eliza would go as to a sacrifice.

"If you died, and I married again, Wick, how would you feel about it? About the man, I mean."

"I'd want to kill the son of a bitch."

"I thought so."

She stood up.

"There's that, too, you see," she said, sharing the tag end of her thought with him.

"What do you mean? My God, when you get to figuring!"

She told him that David was dead five months, and that it was a very natural thing for everything about his life and his memory to be sacred to his mother and the others of his family. All she had left of him was the likeness of him as she had last seen him four years ago, together with the situation in life which had been his at the moment of his death. That situation locked him forever in marriage to Eliza. It might come as a deeply shocking idea to Dorothy that Eliza might want to marry again; as if anybody lived who could ever take the place of David, who was dead so pitiably after their years of valiant confidence and hope. Who could take the responsibility of adding the smallest weight to the sorrows already borne, and borne so well, by their dearest friend? And yet! Yet!

She had her hand on the doorknob.

"Diana, where are you going?"

"I'm going to see Doro a second."

"What are you going to do?"

"What I'd want anyone to do for me."

"What do you mean?"

"Tell me the whole story, if the rest of my life depended on it."

He had an impulse to rise and hold her with his arms. But she was gone. He settled back into his chair shaking his head at the core of her personality. It had delighted him for years, even if on occasions it had also worried him. He had never quite defined it, but without putting it into words he knew what he meant, he meant that she had extraordinary moral energy, along with her other amusing and capable traits, by which he was never alarmed.

xlii

The big square house came awake again at tea time. From outdoors, where the afternoon was still warm, and the light was a melting pale peach color, came a glow that filled the formal drawing room with a mellow twilight. Candles were burning on the mantel-piece and the tables which backed the couches by the fireplace. On each side of the fireplace Vivi had disposed an oleander tree in its tub. These had been brought in from the sun porch where they normally lived. They stood well out of the throw of the heat from the mildly burning logs. In front of each of the two couches which faced each other before the hearth, there was a low table. From one, Vivi served tea. From the other, Dorothy poured coffee. They were near enough so that from her side, Vivi could call introductions of guests across to her sister. There would be plenty of junior officers and midshipmen present to hand around cups and plates and sandwiches and *petit fours*. It was Vivi's belief that they must have this exercise, and that it was a part of her job to tyrannize amiably over them until they could conduct themselves in company as comfortably as they could in gunnery or torpedo practice.

Nobody arrived before half past five; and then as if by signal, crowds of people arrived at about the same time. They had been invited for "five to seven," and with naval coördination, almost everyone had decided that to go at five would seem too eager, and to go at six would be so late as to seem indifferent to the Superintendent's hospitality.

Among the first to come were Commander Morton and Sarah Cleveland. She wore a different costume this time with her plumed hat crowning her handsome head. She wore it as a gesture of self-respectful defiance, and when Phil Morton had groaned at her that she simply couldn't show up like that after what she'd said to Mrs Grace that morning, he'd been told that what she'd said was at his direction, and it had got her into a most disagreeable situation, and if they were to go to tea at the

Admiral's, it would be in her hat, so to speak, or not at all. He knew they had to go; they'd been commanded. But as he followed her into the drawing room, he was most uneasy at what Mrs Grace would think. He decided, when he heard Vivi speak, that he really would never be entirely sure of his idea of her. She put forth her hand to Miss Cleveland, and drew her down on the couch next to her.

"My dear," she said to Sarah, "the fact is that you had a hat all along, but out of some kindly sense of loyalty to our harassed Phillips Morton, you told me a story to justify your having stayed away from Chapel. And now you appear with a perfectly beautiful creation on your head, and I can only admire your honesty in refusing any longer to carry out an insincere position. You must come back and go to Chapel with us another time. And now I would love to give you some tea."

Sarah looked up at Commander Morton standing before her, and gave him an inexpressibly comic look. Then she said to Vivi,

"I am ever so grateful to you, Mrs Grace, for clearing the air so completely. We must now arrange for Phil to take these matters as easily."

This struck Mrs Grace as being a little out of bounds. Phillips Morton, after all, wore the uniform of the United States Navy, and owed a proper concern for everything that took place in the establishment of his chief.

"Not at all," said Vivi, looking at him with a proprietary eye, "I would not have him any different at all from what he is. He is the perfect aide. I have often heard Avy say so. Here is your tea, Phil."

162

He bent down to take it and Sarah could not decide whether he was blushing with pleasure, or whether the firelight was throwing its glow over him.

"You do play the piano, Miss Cleveland," stated Vivi. "Won't you play a little later, when you might feel like it? All the other young people would be so glad if you would. This sort of thing is finally a strain for them, standing up and being so cheekily respectful for hours at a time." She waved her hand. The room by now was full of high rank with a chorus of midshipmen and junior officers. "If you played, they could gather around you. But I think they might even if you didn't." She smiled with one of her slow dazzles at Sarah and inclined her head. It amounted to a dismissal, but such a graceful one that Miss Cleveland could only rise and move away wondering how on earth she could have imagined that Mrs Grace had reproved her this morning. There were others waiting to speak to their hostess. Vivi was surrounded.

Opposite her, Dorothy was equally occupied. Between the sisters, Eliza and Diana and a half dozen youngsters saw to the guests who stood around the room, or sat in the corners, or wandered out to the sun porch where the curtains were still open to the pale twilight which hung in the bare treetops.

It was like a reunion for Dorothy. Old friends sought her out. They wondered how much, if anything, they might say to her of her son David. To those who seemed confused or hesitant, she mentioned him herself—she would say that coming back here was always such a pleasure, and now more particularly than ever, with its memories of her husband and her son; and how fortunate she was that her sister and Avy were here, and could have her come and stay with them. Avy was almost more than her own brother to her. All her life he had helped her in difficulty. And so quietly, too. There was something about his mere presence.

She looked over at him, as he stood talking to Sarah and Phil. The Admiral nodded them on among the guests, and turned to greet some new arrivals, one of whom was a midshipman who seemed to be on the point of both choking to death and dying of thirst, from the way he kept fingering his tight starched color, and licking his dry lips. Avy recognized the panic of the cub who is thrown for the first time into grownup games. He himself took the youngster to meet Vivi, and then to Dorothy when he said he'd rather have coffee, and when the coffee was ready, Avy steered him across the room to where a pretty girl of about the same age was backed up against a sofa by an alcoholic captain who always found the youngest girl in any gathering. Avy captured the girl, with a comradely wink at the captain who was made to seem partner to the Admiral's amiable plot and who could thus only take it and like it. The youngsters were introduced, and Avy then took them across the big room to the piano, where Phil was trying to persuade Sarah to play. Avy said he had a pair of very musical young people with him who would love to hear her play, and then in a stroke of penetration, set Miss Cleveland entirely at ease by adding,

"Go on and play, Miss Sarah. Nobody'll listen to you, since they're all talking. You can have a private little time here all by yourselves."

He clapped the young midshipman on the shoulder, and said, "Delighted you could come, sir," and returned to the other guests, leaving the young man entirely comfortable now, and sworn to him forever.

When Sarah began to play, Vivi lifted her head and recognized the accomplishment of the performance, and was grateful for what it added to her party. Everyone's voice rose, accommodating to the added sound of the piano in the room. The effect heightened the party, almost as if at one stroke. Talk sounded more original and animated against that curtain of music. It was a national habit to enjoy many kinds of noise together. Sarah was playing what she called her African Boogie, which she had perfected during her Red Cross tour in Bengazi. It consisted of playing the rhythm pattern in the right hand instead of the left, and in the left, devising all the melodic variations which the theme suggested. After a few minutes of that, she turned her attention to one of the witty piano preludes of Shostakovich.

There was a common recognition of the moment when the party reached its height. At about half past six, it seemed safe to Vivi to leave her tea table and wander among the others. Nobody had arrived for some time, and some were leaving.

At about this time, Duncan Richards went over and sat down by Dorothy on her sofa. He thought she was unbelievably what—brave? Strong? Tireless? He could not say; but he had watched her during the hour, and her animation, the spontaneity and sincerity of her rediscovery of old friends, the rather thin but sweet expression of her face, moved him. He thought she looked handsome, in a black velvet dress with long sleeves that came down almost to her knuckles like the dress of a princess in a fairy tale, and a diamond bow knot above her heart.

He was white in the face and tired.

He wished he could tell her about the drive with Eliza that afternoon. Eliza had finished things off. She had made him give his word to say nothing.

He realized that it was all on behalf of the woman he sat next to on the couch. He wondered why he didn't dislike her for the disaster she had unwittingly occasioned in his life. But the fact was he did not dislike her. He admired her, and if he were pressed in his thoughts on the subject to know them really clearly, he would have confessed that he even loved her, not passionately, but as a young man can love an older woman when he sees realized in her all the grace, warmth and dignity of which in those of his own age there were merely attractive predictions. And, too, there was much of David in her; and of those other years when they had all been so happy; and no matter what you said about it, the fact was he was forever bound to David's family because of the last days together at Prison Compound Number 2, at Noyashima, on the island of Kusan, southwest of Japan proper.

Dorothy was looking across the room to where Liza was telling some people, including Admiral Richards, about something that required illustration by passing her long white chiffon scarf from one hand to the other several times, after each of which there was a brief pause for moderate laughter, and at the end of which, with the scarf under the arm, and both hands held up to show that they were empty, much delighted laughter. Whatever it was about, Liza did it prettily, and Dorothy's pulse made a beat at the recognition of how stout-hearted the girl was, to be among people so freely, and make them forget their little troubles, and her great one, which must sit upon her like the night, and be dispelled only for a few moments at a time, only to return to its full possession when her mind was not consciously occupied by other things. Dorothy remembered thinking at one time that she had two hearts, full of different kinds of love; one for her husband, one for her son. She had lost them both, and could not speak, if she must, as to which love was the more bitterly lost. Eliza had turned to her before, in her loneliness and sorrow. She would not fail Eliza now.

"Did you have a pleasant drive?" she asked Duncan beside her.

"Oh, very pleasant," he replied, trying to sound light and offhand, in the spirit of his pact with Eliza. But he was a poor actor, and Dorothy looked quickly at him to see if his eyes revealed anything of what made him sound so odd. His face held something she knew she must recognize sooner or later.

She glanced around.

The party was levelled off on a sort of stable progress. It was well launched. Dorothy did not permit anything to darken the pleasure of those around her. Only now, when the day was nearly spent, and there was time for it without casting a shadow upon anyone, did she ask to be told at last what she had come to hear.

"Duncan, will you go up to my sitting room with me? There is so much you have to tell me."

Nobody was really aware that Dorothy and Lieutenant Richards left the party except Vivi. She saw them go, and she was sure she knew why they were going. Without revealing feeling in the presence of the guests she was talking to, she felt her heart go heavy, and she wished with all her might that she could take Dorothy's place, whom she would spare whatever she could. But she knew there was nothing anybody else could do about it; and with a thought that was like a blessing, she let them go.

xliii

In the upstairs sitting room which was next to her bedroom, Dorothy closed the door after Duncan and locked it, explaining that guests might otherwise blunder in here and interrupt them.

There was a little fire going in the grate. One lamp was lighted, on a table between the windows that looked out toward the river. On the chimney-piece there was a green leather folding frame containing two photographs. They were of Hoppy and David, both in uniform. These photographs travelled everywhere with Dorothy.

She asked Duncan to sit down opposite her. The fireplace was between them. The room was in deep twilight. A soft evening was darkening outside. She leaned forward to take a cigarette from a painted Mexican box on the little low table before the hearth. He leaped up and lighted it for her.

"I have not smoked for years," she said, with a smile. He sat down again. He clasped his hands tightly. She leaned forward. His agitation was painful. Each was feeling sympathy for the other.

"Duncan, do you mind telling me how it—?"

He ducked his head to signify no.

After a moment he began to speak, hardly looking at her at first. He talked rapidly, without dramatics, but, once he was started, with a sort of brutal urgency that made him crowd image after image and detail upon detail into his account. His eyes began to burn. They seemed to sink into their sockets a little, as he drew down his brows to frown a terrible life into his inner vision. He did not remain seated for long at a time. He got up and at moments he bent over her and gazed intently into her face. She faced up to him. She looked haggard. Valor and pretense were gone. Every word he spoke stripped her of the aspect she had worn so long for the comfort of the world around her. He saw the tears come into her eyes once or twice; but they seemed to be instantly consumed by the hunger and heat of her gaze. He walked away from her and came back. He paced the room. When he would glance at her he would see that even in the firelight she seemed to become whiter and whiter in the face. He could imagine the shock of his story. He wished he had graces with which to give her the essential truth without assaulting her with it; but his bitter thoughts came so turbulently, his memories were so possessive, that he found himself in their power as he released them.

Once he paused, for he thought she might be going to faint. She put her hand to her eyes. In a moment she nodded to him to continue, and he felt that she was making a supreme effort to finish now what they had both undertaken. If she let him stop now, God only knew when she might have the strength to undertake this again. He licked his lips and resumed. His voice was sandy and ugly with emotion. He told his story with order, simply following the sequence of events as he had encountered them.

Faintly, below, were the sounds of the party; Miss Cleveland's piano, the damped shrillness of the conversation, the occasional tremor deep in the house as the big front door closed after someone leaving.

Neither Dorothy nor Duncan was aware of such sounds. But as he talked, the things he was describing made an appalling contrast to the civility of the life which was implicit in the house and its history.

xliv

The two young classmates did not serve together at all during the war, and wrote to each other infrequently. From the hospital in Manila after being wounded, before his capture, David did write Duncan a letter full of nonsense and cockiness which hardly concealed a deep gloom over the severity of his wounds and the partial paralysis of his left arm. Actually, reading the letter, Duncan had made up his mind that David was dead, and that there would never be a factual report of his fate.

In June, 1945, Duncan, with several hundred other American Navy prisoners of the Japanese, was brought by steamer to the island of Kusan. The voyage had been hideous. Duncan survived it mainly by the grim thought that however dreadful the prison life might be at their destination, it could not be as bad as the prison ship. He was inclined to change his guess later. He was placed with other Navy officer personnel in Prison Compound Number 2, at Noyashima. The night he arrived he was stricken with a high fever and was unconscious for nearly a week. He was ignored by the Japanese authorities, and never had a call from the prison camp doctor. An American Navy doctor in his group nursed him. When he recovered his awareness, he could not believe he had been gone for so many days from the world. It was a world bitter to return to. The doctor let him move around a little the first day, but made him play unconscious when the Japanese lieutenant in charge of their billet—Lieutenant Ika—came around; for if he had seen that Duncan was awake, he would have ordered him to his feet, to make the obeisances required of all prisoners, and then would have assigned him to a work detail, which might have killed him. In a few days the doctor could no longer risk keeping him down for fear that his weakness would grow instead of recede. He had to let him up, and he was immediately told what he must do.

He must go to the long narrow enclosure marked off by barbed wire barriers so thick that they resembled hedges, and there stand at attention from now until the Japanese corporal in charge said he might fall out. New to such ways, he tried to find out why he was being disciplined. He was informed in pantomime and broken English that it was because he had been absent from his duties for a week. He reminded the corporal that he had been ill and unable to report. This was regarded as insolence, and for it, the corporal casually knocked him down with the butt of his rifle, then kicked him to get up again, and prodded him to get in line with eleven other American prisoners who were already at attention staring into the sunlight.

They stood there for about two and a half hours. At last, one

171

of their number fainted and the suggestibility of this was so great that three more fainted in rapid succession. The remaining prisoners were ordered to pick up their fellows and carry them around and around the enclosure until they should revive, while the guards observed the procedure without visible opinion. Duncan never knew why in his weakened condition he had not fainted; but he assumed that as a recent captive, and a fairly late arrival, he had not reached that degree of semi-starvation which was the ordinary lot of the inmates of the Noyashima compounds. He carried the head and shoulders of one of the unconscious prisoners, and a tall, skeletal young officer carried the feet. They went round and round he knew not how many times. They were it seemed on the very brink of collapse when the ordeal was ended by the call to lunch for the Japanese guards. The absurd march stopped, the prisoners were dismissed and told to return to their barracks, and the guards departed, which they could do safely from their own point of view because the enclosure was within the camp area and prisoners could not escape casually. Duncan and his partner laid their burden down and flopped to the ground themselves. When he got his breath a little, he leaned over to see if the man they'd been carrying was coming to properly. He saw that his sunken eyes were opened, and his bearded mouth was dry, and that he seemed to be recovering himself.

"Come on, if you can get up, we'll go back to the barracks, and maybe find you a drink of water."

The other man closed his eyes and shook his head. He spoke in a hesitant, husky voice.

"No water. They don't let you have it except at each meal."

There was nothing to be said at this point, so they rested a while longer. And then by common consent, arose, and began to walk with the gaunt and jerky walk of skeletons back toward their own area.

Duncan meant to walk beside his recent charge, who, however, hung back, walking more slowly, and they arrived at the barracks separately. He wanted to talk to the other prisoner, for there was some sort of bond set up between them by the cruel and senseless episode of the morning. After a while he walked down the big room in the raw plank barracks where all the bunks were, looking for him. Toward the opposite end from his own bunk, he found the man he was searching for, lying on his bunk, and staring as he approached. His eyes were burning with an eloquent expression, and in their sunken sockets, in that skull-like face, with its blond beard, which was neatly trimmed, they seemed to be full of silent messages. Duncan came and sat down on the edge of the bunk. The man on the bed rolled his head from side to side several times, and then Duncan realized that there was a smile on that face, and he felt a hand reach to his knee, and heard a thin husky voice say,

"You never knew me, Deedy."

He felt as if someone had struck him in the chest with a club. He leaned down and stared. There was only one man in the world who called him that. It was David Hopkinson. Duncan pulled him up and wrung his hands and held him by the shoulders.

It seemed that as they walked back from the enclosure that morning, David had struggled in his hunger-clouded mind to recognize Duncan, and when he finally did, he was saddened by the fact that Duncan obviously had not known him. This proved to David how terribly he had changed. He had hung back, reluctant to talk with this stranger who did not know his best friend.

"It is the beard, of course," said Duncan.

David closed his eyes and shook his head. He even smiled over it now. He said nonsense. He knew what he looked like. He didn't blame Duncan. As for the beard, for years he like all the others had shaved every day. They treasured their razor-blades and sharpened them over and over, because it was a point of honor with them as officers to keep their appearance up despite the foulest assignments the guards could give them. Nobody ever knew why the Japanese let them keep the blades. But the fact was, and David admitted it with an apologetic look, he had become too weak to shave every day, to stand there and hold up his arms even for the little time it took. That much rest gave him just the little extra energy he needed to be able to meet the demands made upon him along with the other prisoners. He had looked odd the first couple of months with his whiskers; but then they sort of took hold, and grew consistently, and one of the fellows—the doctor—had a pair of scissors and once a week he trimmed David's beard and mustache for him, so it would look deliberate, an airy gesture on his part, to have grown them.

Duncan gave him all the news he could. He himself had been captured only a month before. He could report on the war. Europe had fallen. The Pacific fleet was raiding Japan itself with monster demonstrations of power. The Army Air Forces with their B-29s—were bombing Japan from bases that moved nearer and nearer. He swore to David that the war must end in a very few months, with an Allied victory. He said

174

they must hang on for all they were worth; after going this far they could not fail to make it the rest of the way. David coughed before he could answer. His enthusiasm and emotion choked him. He said he believed, and the doctor did too, that he had a touch of something in one lung, but they hadn't noticed it getting worse lately, so perhaps it'd turn out all right.

Their discovery of each other was one of the marvels of the barracks for the next few days. But the doctor soberly warned them not to display their old intimacy and mutual interest to the guards, or they would be separated and whatever pleasure and sustenance they got from each other's company would be taken from them.

Duncan talked privately to the doctor about David. Yes, he undoubtedly had tuberculosis, not necessarily incurable. His arm was fairly useful, though it tired easily. His temper had improved lately, which relieved the doctor of one worry, for David ran fewer risks now of extraordinary punishments than he used to receive, because he could not resist a show of disdain, disgust or amusement at the Japanese methods of handling prisoners. In view of forecasts brought by the new prisoners of how soon the war might end, the doctor thought that David would pull through. He believed that Duncan's presence would be as powerful an aid as anything.

For a few days Duncan could not understand what seemed to be periods of vagueness and indifference in David, when he would seem barely to recognize him, and to have drifted into a world of thoughts and interests far away. And then he thought he detected in himself a similar tendency, and he consulted the doctor, who told him that this attitude was the result of under-nourishment and nagging hunger. Complete, effective consciousness simply did not exist for most of the prisoners. They seemed to awaken to their circumstances only at odd moments.

But when they went on work details, Duncan tried to arrange that he be next to David as they marched, or as they worked in the enclosure, or at cleaning latrines which they were forced to do with their bare hands, without brushes or cloths.

In late afternoon and early evening before the light was gone, they had a few free moments. They wrote letters to everyone at home, and amused themselves and each other by devising clever ways to tell the truth about prison conditions without actually saying outright what the Japanese might understand. "Oh, boy, Leavenworth was never like this," was supposed to indicate obliquely that things were far worse in Japanese prisons. They supposed that few letters and postcards ever reached their destinations. But the prisoners would faith-fully write them and plod over to the orderly room of the camp headquarters to "mail" them.

One night a fortnight after Duncan arrived, he went in the last twilight to mail letters with David. An electric light was burning in the orderly room. They could hear the put-put-put of the camp dynamo in the distance. A short fat soldier was on duty. They held their letters to him. He knocked them to the board floor, and indicated that they were to pick them up and lay them on the table. They leaned down. He pushed their heads and they fell back on their haunches. He kicked them for being so clumsy and made them get up. He pulled their shirts out of their waists and leered, taking satisfaction from this destruction of their wretched neatness. Then he took a cigarette from a packet that had the American Red Cross sticker pasted over its top. The packet had been stolen from a carton consigned to American prisoners of war. He put the cigarette into his mouth, and lighted a match, and in the flame he held the letters they had brought. When these were burning brightly, he lighted his cigarette from them, and then threw the burning envelopes futilely at David and Duncan. The papers curled into black ash at their feet. The soldier sat down at his table. They started to turn and go. He ordered them to remain and to stand at attention. He kept them standing there for an hour. Every time they made a move, an inadvertant trembling, or any such, he squinted at them menacingly. Finally he turned them out into the pitch darkness. No light showed. Prisoner barracks were not allowed illumination. They had to feel their way, crawling most of the distance, back to their barracks. It was a cold night. But when after what seemed an interminable journey they arrived at the wooden step to their squad room they had a shaming sense of relief. They were sweating in panic from the darkness, the humiliation in the orderly room, and indeed from the very degradation which they saw in themselves, that they should return to those barracks as if to home, safety and self-respect.

That night David coughed more than he slept. His arm which was his pillow was flecked with little points of blood in the morning. But he arose with the rest, marched to breakfast, and afterward was sent out to the far corner of the compound, nearest the small mountains of the island, to dig his hole for the day. Each man had a hole. When it was dug, he was to fill it in again. Neatness was required. The finest hole was that which when filled in showed no sign of having been dug. One or two prisoners, fanatical in their glaring thought of surviving at any cost whatever, actually worked to please the guards, bringing bits of grass and crusts of earth in order to finish their refilled holes with ingenious camouflage.

It was pretty nice how all the others did what they could to ease David's plight. The trouble was that you never knew when one of the guards or Lieutenant Ika might show up. It wasn't long till the authorities observed that his fellow prisoners were favoring Lieutenant Hopkinson. The inevitable consequence was that the authorities invented things to do which would be harmful to him. Lieutenant Ika stated in formal and limited English that the compound was a democracy, and that no one, whether lieutenant or lieutenant-commander, was to be given privileges of any sort, even by his fellow prisoners. They all got a bitter laugh out of his mouthing of democracy, and decided it was the painful process of the Oriental who, despising the values of the powerful Occidentals, yet had to ape them, to gain face. The reëstablishment of democracy in the compound was demonstrated by the order that on days when David was too weak to go to work or to drill or to hole-digging with the rest of them, he was to be carried out by the others, and laid on the ground in the sunlight, to be with them while they did their duties. He suffered intensely from the sunlight, having to be inactive in it. A foreseeable result of the order was that to save his fellows any trouble he made superhuman efforts to go and take care of himself. The doctor would rage in private at the treatment, but was powerless, and knew it. He kept saying if only David could have even a little nourishing food. . . .

One day a happy thrill ran through the camp. The prisoners had seen two trucks roll up and though they were ordered into their quarters, there to stay away from the windows, they could see enough to know that the trucks brought Prisoner of War cartons from the Red Cross. It meant food, cigarettes, candy. It meant little symptoms of home, in the mechanical expertness of the packaging, and even in the printed matter on the cans and packets and wrappers. The prisoners were frantic with eagerness. They organized a committee to go and tell the camp commander, who was called The Major, that they had seen the cartons arrive, and respectfully requested that the committee be permitted to administer the distribution. If they'd been strong and in their full senses they would never have made such a move. Duncan was a member of the committee. The Major pointed at him and said "Troubber-maker!" and dismissed them without an answer.

An answer came soon enough. While they were kept in quarters during one whole day, the prisoners watched a detachment of camp guards rip open all the cartons and take each can of food and pierce it with a bayonet. Late that afternoon, the prisoners were formed, and told that the Red Cross had shipped supplies to them, which the authorities were pleased to turn over to them. They cried with rage. They would get one day's good meals, or maybe two, from that wealth of stuff, before it spoiled. Left properly, it would have sustained them for months. They went out and with tears of fury on their faces they gathered their mutilated boxes and went back to barracks. There they found the cigarettes had all been withheld.

They had a bad night of it. It rained. Their thoughts were like the rain, falling and falling through their wakeful minds.

In the morning the cigarettes were brought out before a formation of the prisoners. It was announced that the men might have the cigarettes upon dismissal. At that point, the guards ripped the cartons with knives and scattered the torn packets in the puddles left by the rain. Desperately the prisoners broke ranks and tried to salvage the cigarettes. Most of the packets were soaked through; but they gathered them up to dry them out in the sun and smoke them later. David managed to get his arms full, and the guards permitted this; but when he tried putting more packets into his shirt, something about it struck them as unsuitable, and one of the guards slapped him.

He fell down.

His packets scattered, some back into the puddles again. The sight was too much for a lieutenant-commander who was nearby. He was a big man, still ruddy, shaggily bearded with dark hair which concealed some of his emaciation. He had nostrils like a bull. They flared now. He lost his head. He leaped at the guard who had slapped David, and struck him a solid blow in the face. The guard fell back, and the prisoner struck him again. The other prisoners were now tugging at him to hurry him off before any more could happen. It was no use. In a couple of seconds the other guards had him. Some orders were shouted. Fighting and roaring, a spectacle of an absurd but magnificent extravagance of life itself, the lieutenant-commander was dragged across the area and tied by his wrists to a low hydrant and made to kneel. The guards then formed a semi-circle around him at a few paces, and at another order, fired a volley that killed him at once.

His body was left there for two days. The prisoners were forbidden to go near it. In his last position, he was bent over and crumpled, his knees under him, his forehead to the earth, in a spurious humility which made his comrades bitter when they looked across the windswept area at him. Six men from the barracks were told off to bury him at last. One of these, cleverly chosen, was David. He wanted to make an open and outrageous rebellion himself, just like the man who had avenged the affront to him. They all tried to soothe him. Duncan reminded him of Eliza and his mother. He knew, he knew; but would they want him as he now was? Such a thought was a gauge of his illness.

He talked of Eliza and Dorothy constantly. When he and Duncan had their free moments, they wrote letters and cards, and sometimes talked of their old days. David loved to recall the days of his youth in New Mexico. He used to speak of the open country, the mountains so persuasive of some desire for the horizon, and the freedom he always felt there. It was that image of freedom to which his mind turned in captivity. He recalled the summer fishing trip on which Deedy had gone with him that time, with Commander Hopkinson. He vowed to Deedy that they would go back together some day, and do it all over again, in the same places.

It was an odd thing, but David, who'd never been particularly expressive before, but had been known and loved for his fine presence, and his smiling response to people, was now able with an almost poetic concentration and effect to recall and make Duncan see the very sights, sounds, flavors of times past. It was like dreaming aloud and conducting someone else into your dream. It fascinated Duncan even while it scared him. He thought the vitality of that vision was something no mortal could long endure to contain. It consumed David. But there was as much momentary happiness in his burning looks as there was disease. Duncan could not discourage him.

In July a Swedish inspector for the Red Cross came to survey the compounds and make his report. He was going first to inspect Noyashima Compound Number 1, which was for United States Army prisoners. That would take the morning. In the afternoon he would be in Number 2. The Major would show him around. The prisoners were to be in the barracks. Lieutenant Ika appointed a spokesman for each barracks. The doctor would speak for David's. He was instructed to give a good report. Ika believed that with one exception this group of prisoners would look creditable. The exception was David. He ordered him removed. Duncan begged to go with him. He was refused. David was hauled away no one knew where.

The inspector came, a stout, florid man with a hurried manner, which seemed perhaps more like guilt than haste or indifference. He was probably moved and appalled by what he saw, but he knew he was powerless to force any improvement. He would make his report. He could not get away fast enough from the indignities which were perfectly plain, despite the Major's attempt to present everything in a good light. The inspector asked the doctor if they had received any Red Cross cartons lately. The doctor was obliged to say yes. He was about to add the circumstances, when he saw Ika's face and he knew that a reckless indulgence in the truth would bring reprisals not only upon himself but upon everyone else. He shut up.

"You really received them?" insisted the inspector. The whole squad room could hear.

"Yes."

With a wretched sigh the Swedish inspector passed on to the next man. Late in the afternoon, they all heard his airplane soaring off from the landing field to the south, where the beach levelled toward a long, flat, green meadow that ran to the base of the mountains five miles inland. His visit and his departure were a matter of the utmost cynicism to the prisoners.

They all wondered for days what had happened to David. Was he dead? Or hidden in the infirmary which was equipped with medical and surgical supplies, but never used for the prisoners, only for the camp garrison?

But one day they brought him back. A little stronger, he was amused at his experience. He had been put in a tent at the airfield, and fed by a little Japanese soldier who had once been a bellboy in the Palace Hotel in San Francisco. Once out of sight of his superiors, the bellboy delighted to play at being a Yank, and improvised all sorts of excellent service, extra food and comforts, to prove his skill. He would sit for hours, "guarding" David, but lost in a rhapsody of delight, describing the lobby, the court, the indoor balconies, the stained glass, the elevators, the kitchens, the grand dining rooms, the men's washroom, the furnace room, of the Palace Hotel. He said he was going right straight back there after the war was over.

David asked how could he? The United States wouldn't take any Japanese in for a long time. He replied that he meant when Japan won the war, as she was so plainly doing right now.

Duncan was so much encouraged by David's improvement through his days of hiding away in the tent, and of eating relatively better food, that he wanted to do everything possible to preserve the gain. It became his practice in the mess hall to hide morsels of food inside his shirt and bring them to David in the evening to eat when the darkness was falling, and the long bare planked barrack room was mercifully disappearing in shadows. The morsels were hardly better than crumbs, but in that scarcity, every calorie was precious. He had some trouble persuading David that he must accept these gifts. But by dwelling upon the medical aspects of the case, he succeeded. In fact, and it touched him more deeply than many more rugged circumstances of the imprisonment, David in his weakness and exhaustion could not conceal a little greed, once he had been persuaded to accept the extra food; a sort of spoiled hunger for privilege which made him sulk if on any evening Duncan was unable to bring his usual tribute. It was a fact that did not discredit David. Men were so readily and so pitifully reduced to animals when humanity's values were outraged.

One evening Lieutenant Ika suddenly appeared in the barracks near David's bunk. He caught David eating. He sent for additional guards with lanterns. They brought two electric flashlights and six paper lanterns of a festive character. The childish beauty of these, the associations of innocent gaiety which Japanese lanterns held for Americans, made some of the prisoners choke on their childhood memories. Ika ordered everyone to strip and stand at attention at the foot of the bunks. He conducted an inspection. If anyone was carrying food he would discover evidence. The inspection took nearly an hour. Nothing was found. But Ika stood and stared fixedly into Duncan's eyes for what seemed like five minutes. Then he spat upon his bare flesh and strode down the squad room, and ordered David to pick up his clothes and march. The guards closed around him. He walked out of the barracks with his khakis over his arm, coughing. He turned and waved as he went through the door, smiling as if the joke was on the Japanese. Then the lanterns were gone, and they all believed he was being taken away to be shot. Duncan was ready to die himself, for he believed it to be his fault that David had been caught breaking imaginary rules.

For weeks they heard nothing, but as each day went by without the sound of a firing squad, or the educational display of David's dead body, the prisoners took heart. He turned up in late July, explaining that he had been moved to Noyashima Compound Number 1, among the U. S. Army prisoners. The Japanese had evidently figured out an elaborate belief that as he was a Navy man, if they put him permanently among Army men, he would be starved, snubbed and persecuted. The fact was the opposite. He was generously handled by the Army prisoners. They had a different diet, no better, just different. The change was enough to make him ill for several days. While he was laid up over there, a chaplain, Father John Zabriski, a Pole from Buffalo, New York, struck up an acquaintance, and helped him. The fact was that Father Zabriski did so many good things for David, that after a while of it, the Japanese ordered him returned to the Navy compound.

185

Duncan was overjoyed to have him back and see him no worse. But the change back to the Number 2 compound diet made him ill again. He had dysentery. About the same time, some tainted food was distributed, and many of the prisoners came down with food poisoning, including Duncan. They were many days recovering their minimal strength. Lieutenant Ika came in and called them to attention and made a long speech reproaching them for a complete lack of sense of duty. So much work to be done. Nobody doing it. He made it plain that he believed them all malingerers of the worst sort. He announced a new policy. The discipline had up to now been lenient and considerate, but now he and the Major were at the end of their patience, sick and tired of having their forbearance abused by these indifferent and impolite Americans. There would be no more tolerance of laxness of any sort. This was just a fatherly warning.

Actually, the authorities were affronted because the prisoners survived as well as they did. It seemed to indicate a superiority that was thoughtless and innate, a grasp of life that depended upon some secret unknown to the Japanese, which infuriated them.

There were immediate consequences of the new policy, all of them painful to their victims. The one Duncan spoke of was that which affected David. It was this. David had to be assisted to the outdoor latrines, to which his dysentery made him have recourse very often. Each time, one of his friends hauled him by slow steps and with supporting arms, over the clear space

186

behind the barracks. He was grateful; but he was also impatient and humiliated. One moonlit night he gritted his jaw, got up and went outside trembling on his legs, determined to go alone this time. He was returning to the barracks slowly, barely able to stand for dizziness and weakness, when a guard came over from his post at the barbed wire barriers, and nudged him to get going faster. David tried, but fell to his knees. The guard hauled him to his feet again, and, sanctioned by the new policy, prodded him with his bayonet to make him get moving. David started forward again, went a few steps, and again faltered to his knees. This time the guard thrust the bayonet into his left arm an inch or so, and then dragged him along the ground to the barrack door and with much fumbling breathy cursing got him inside and left him on the floor. The moonlight rested upon him through the screen. Someone came to help him get to his bunk. He was unconscious until morning. His wound was discovered when the light came in the sky. That was the beginning of the end.

By evening the bayonet wound was hotly infected, and the doctor was watching for gangrene, as the circulation of David's left arm had been impaired by the earlier wounds in the Battle of Manila.

The doctor went to see the Major and described the case. He begged for a light to use overnight so he could watch his patient; and for medicines, a hypodermic needle and drugs— all these things were needed at once, and he feared other supplies might be needed later.

The Major referred to the recently announced policy, and stated that it was unfortunate that this had to happen now; if it had happened before the new policy, he might well have been able to accede to such requests. So far as he could see, for the present, he was powerless.

The doctor said he might rescind the policy as he had made it in the first place.

The camp commander became infuriated at this; drew himself up, and declared that it was an *official* policy, made so by his own promulgation; his authority came from the Emperor through the chain of command; who was to trifle with that?

It was all the doctor could do to refrain from violence. He gloomily went back to the barracks.

By the next day it was clear that gangrene had made fast progress during the night. The doctor knew that the only thing to do was amputate. He told Duncan so, and set him to watch David, for as long as he could, until time for work formation, when he would have to go, or suffer God only knew what new inventions of indignity.

Then the doctor went back to the Major and took a new tack. He begged leave to discuss a matter of much urgency that had him baffled. He was a trained surgeon and a naval officer, and had had many and various cases. But if he might presume to say so, he was baffled, and came for advice?

The camp commander was impassive. He nodded to continue.

The doctor then did an elaborate recital, in pantomime, simplified English, and even with a few scholarly looking diagrams drawn on the Major's desk pad, of what developed when a wound turned poisonous, and generated gangrene. Did he have the right to make a decision? On the one hand, et cetera, et cetera; and on the other, so-and-so, and so-and-so. The Major was an officer of much position and great experience. As a matter of command decision, what would he recommend?

Thoughtful interval.

The Major's eyes seemed to become more liquid. Otherwise not a shadow of thought affected his face. But the doctor felt his own heart beating fast with excitement at the tiny change in the Japanese officer's eyes, for he had reached through to that idiot vanity, and maybe there was a chance; a chance.

At last the Major rested his hands upon the hilt of his sword and leaned sociably forward, to announce his decision. He stated that though not a man of medicine he was like all sound Japanese officers trained in every field that had to do with maintenance of men. He perceived the dilemma which perplexed the American doctor, but he said that it would not for a moment puzzle a Japanese Imperial officer.

No? said the doctor in enchanted wonder.

No, said the Major.

Then what is the decision?

The camp commander made an exquisitely delicate little gesture across his left biceps, indicating "to amputate." The doctor could hardly restrain his inner exultation. But he only leaned forward, let his jaw drop, and clasped his hands together in gratitude. He nodded and stood up.

"I will!" he said.

The Major leaned back a trifle and made a bleak little smile which was all his pride would allow him. The doctor started out, and then snapped his fingers as if he had nearly forgotten something.

He turned back and said that in that case, the Major having given the order, which he greatly appreciated, he would have

189

to request certain small facilities to carry it out. He would like to use the infirmary to operate in, and borrow whatever instruments, anesthetic, and so on, might be available. He was casual, as if this would all be implicit in the Major's wise solution of the original dilemma.

Now the doctor had to witness a struggle between vanity and the new policy.

It ended with each factor of the Major's position making a concession. *Vanity* said magnificently that the instruments and supplies would be available. *The new policy* said the infirmary could not be used, only the barracks room.

It was better than the doctor had dared hope for, and he bowed thoughtfully as if this were another brilliant stroke by a master of staff thinking. Then he brightened and said with the confidence one reveals to an intelligent superior, that he would not be able to attend formations himself, during the first few days of the operation and after.

The Major vetoed this. He could be absent half the time.

The doctor said that was reasonable, after all. Why couldn't he have another man absent half the time, and take turns with him?

This suggestion appeared to be an elaboration of the Major's own cleverness, and as such, it was approved.

So it was understood: for the operation, he would have all he needed?

Yes.

Then he would go right now to the infirmary to get the things, if the Major would be so kind as to give him an escort with orders accordingly.

It was done.

The doctor was sweating from what had been an ordeal of wits.

He made his preparations all afternoon, with Duncan's help. Duncan himself told David what needed to be done.

David's fever was high, and the news struck him as dimly interesting. He smiled politely.

They improvised everything; but by nightfall it was over. The one thing David had begged just beforehand, was that Duncan might give him the ether. He didn't know why. It just gave him more confidence. Duncan did it. He was never able to explain how he managed it, for he was trembling so within that he thought he must spill the can of ether rather than let it go, drop by drop.

There was much to worry them at best. The doctor did not like the risk of using ether with a patient whose lungs were affected. But he calculated that the risk was less great in that than the shock which would accompany operating under local anesthetic which might not be totally effective.

The morning after the operation, the camp medical officer came in to look at the patient. He desired that the dressings be removed for his benefit. The Navy doctor was reluctant to do this, and said so. The Japanese doctor did not argue. He simply bent over and began to pull roughly at the bandages. It hurt David considerably and he swore at the man. The American doctor pushed him away and finished unwrapping the dressings himself, exposing the raw stump. For a minute the camp medical officer looked at it, and then walked out, saying nothing.

But later in the day there was a repetition of the episode, when Lieutenant Ika arrived to inspect the patient, and demanded the same privilege as that enjoyed by the camp medical director. He indicated that as officer in charge of this barracks, he especially should enjoy all official information pertaining to it. He departed soon after his official prerogative had been satisfied by another painful undressing of the arm.

An hour or so later the Major appeared on the same mission. His own doctor, and his officer in charge of these barracks, both subordinate to him, had inspected the patient; how could the American doctor have failed so gravely in a matter of the simplest courtesy, not to have invited the camp commander himself to be the first to see the case? And especially since the Major had coöperated so kindly throughout? Once again the bandages were taken off.

That exhausted the run of official vanities. David was allowed to go to sleep without more interruption. The doctor wondered if he would ever wake.

Late the next day he had the first premonition of further trouble. He told Duncan about it. Pneumonia was surely developing. They took turns all night sitting in the dark by David's bunk listening to his hard breathing. By morning there was no longer any doubt. He could not live long. He had times of perfect lucidity when though too weak to speak with any energy, he could manage to order his thoughts and speak them softly, with a smiling and somehow exquisite lightness of breath, as if he knew that to tap more than the shallowest of his powers would be fatal.

Three things happened that morning which Duncan would never forget.

The first was when David seemed to come perfectly awake through his tortured discomfort, to turn his head, look at Duncan who was staying with him while the doctor went out to work, and ask if he was not dying. Duncan said what nonsense, of course he was not dying. David said oh, yes he was. He put his right hand over toward Duncan but could not reach him, but it was the ghost of a comforting gesture, and its grace, its responsibility for the ease of others, was one of the most beautiful things Duncan ever saw. It reminded him of David's mother. David then went back to sleep for a little while.

The second thing was when Duncan, sitting by the bunk, reading the fine print on one of the rain-soaked and dried American cigarette packets, heard something that made him raise his head and listen again. It was a powerful drone far away in the sky. He went to the window and stared upward until he could see an immense formation of bombers. Their engines were beating toward the northeast, toward Japan. The sun flashed off the silver wings. They were United States planes. He recognized them high as they were. It was the clear portent for which they had all been longing.

He went to the bunk and awakened David. News of the flight would help to cure him or to let him die happily.

"David, wake up! Listen! Out the window!"

David looked at him like a little child, drowsily, sweetly, mindlessly content to be nurtured and cared for.

Duncan patted his good arm lightly but urgently.

"David, there is a big formation of American bombers going

over. Can't you hear them? Listen! They are on their way to Japan. It can't be long now. We'll all make it together!"

David turned his head toward the window. The growling in the sky was still audible. In a moment he caught it. He struggled to sit up. He broke into a rickety smile, and made silent but passionate rooting gestures with his mouth and his hand, like any American at a game, backing a team that deserved to win. He was in that moment very much in the spirit of his father. He lay back again and his eyes were lighted by a new hope. It was all true, then. The big planes were passing out of sight and sound. He fell asleep again. Duncan went to the door of the squad room. He could look down the street of the next barracks, beyond which the prisoners were working in a large flower garden maintained for the Major, who was an amateur botanist. Duncan could see their excitement, even from this distance. Most of them would never have been able to identify the B-29s, but the later prisoners who had arrived with Duncan did it for them. They were slapping each other on the back; lifting their arms to the sky; a few very faint rebel yells travelled on the morning breeze; miniature signs of a joy almost too big for their starved bodies and spirits to contain safely.

The third thing was when David awoke again and asked Duncan to arrange for Father Zabriski to come from the other compound and prepare him for death. At this Duncan dropped all his loyal and scornful pretense that David was going to live, not die. He nodded and said he would see about it the minute the doctor came back from the fields. David went to sleep again.

When the prisoners came in for noon mess, Duncan told the

194

doctor what David wanted. They were both afraid that it was an impossible request. But they agreed that the doctor, having had some success with the Major, should try to arrange this matter, rather than Duncan, who had been branded as a "troubber-maker." Accordingly, the doctor went to the headquarters after lunch.

His reception was grim. The splendid and menacing flight of bombers which had gone over in the morning remained with the Major as a personal affront. He was in a doubtful mood also from the episode of the bandages two days before. Nevertheless, he suffered his visitor. His hand was resting on his desk. He indicated with his lifted forefinger that the doctor was to speak.

The doctor told him the young officer whose arm had been amputated was going to die.

The Major stated that he could have told the doctor that two days ago.

The doctor humbly marvelled at this prescience. Then he said he had a problem to discuss which made the conversation of the other day seem trivial.

The Major waited.

The doctor said that in all his experience, in every part of the world, as a professional man, and an officer, the thing that had perhaps struck him as the most impressive of all was the gallantry which gentlemen of the profession of arms bore toward their adversaries when they had them at last helpless. This was true of the British, with their noble lords; the French, with their men of intellect; the Germans, with their high-born military genius; the Americans, with their great technical

195

energy. No doubt the Major had noticed the selfsame thing? Surely it was true of the Imperial Japanese officer corps?

A shrug of agreement.

Well, the doctor proceeded, since as a gentleman (he did not use the word he was thinking of and playing against, which was snob), he and the Major had this professional point of view, the doctor felt much easier about asking what he had come to ask; for a moment—he smiled that he should ever have doubted the Major's powers of understanding—for a moment he had been troubled for fear not of the Major's worldly good breeding, but of his own inability to express himself. But it was plain that he had only to make the barest reference to what was in the wind, for the Major to grasp it instantly.

Well?—without commitment, but with a sense between the two of them that the Major had been jockeyed into the loser's position, and knew it.

The doctor asked that Father John Zabriski, a prisoner in the Noyashima Compound Number 1, be brought to this camp only long enough to afford the consolations of his religion to Lieutenant David Hopkinson, and to bury him after he died according to the rites of the Roman Catholic Church. Here was a slip of paper with Chaplain Zabriski's name written down on it.

The request, so simple, so different from whatever it was he might have expected, made the Major suspicious for a moment. But since the request had been made of him as an international gentleman, compounded of British nobility, French intelligence, German military genius, and American energy, not to mention Imperial Japanese code, there was little he could do but accede. He took up the scrap of paper and said the chaplain would be brought from the other camp immediately. Was that all?

All? The doctor shrugged as one would shrug in saying, My dear fellow, only the most princely of men can make such gestures without ever weighing their cost; saluted; and returned to his barracks.

When they told David that his friend Father Zabriski was being sent for, he seemed to make a start toward recovery. He remained conscious for most of the afternoon, and there was even a little show of natural color in his cheeks. The doctor shook his head, and vowed that if he had anything like the proper medicines, he might pull him through even at that.

In the middle of the afternoon Father Zabriski arrived. He was a tall man, thin like the rest of the prisoners, except that you felt he had always been thinner than most people. His head had a boyish shape, probably because his thick black hair was cropped until it fitted him like a cap. His face was tanned, but the natural whiteness of his skin seemed to show through. Under black brows his dark brown eyes were startling. The pupils were large, so that very little white showed around them in his gaze. There were deep lines in his face. He seemed tired and unwell, until you talked to him; and then he gave a sense of vitality and a reserve of strength. He wore the khaki shirt and slacks of the Army, with his captain's bars and cross on his open collar. He carried a little metal box rolled up in a long strip of worn violet silk.

They brought him to the bunk where David lay frowning in his sleep. The priest glanced from David to the doctor. He had seen much of death, and knew its every premonition. Rapidly he unrolled his package. The violet silk was his stole, which he put around his neck. The little box contained his pyx. He had a vial of holy oil, and a fragment of the unleavened wafer that became the Host. Painfully, for he was sore from his labors at the other camp, Captain Zabriski knelt down beside David and touched his brow, speaking his name. He spoke it twice before David awoke, and turned his head to see who called; but his vision came with difficulty from far away, and he struggled in his brow to make his mind serve him. The chaplain said that it was his old friend Zabriski from the Army compound. He said that he was touched and happy that if anybody was wanted right now, he had been sent for.

"Do you hear me, David? David Hopkinson? I must have you hear me, and answer me. We have a piece of work to do together, David. Will you answer me?"

David's face cleared as if with the idea of Oh yes, of course. He smiled and tried to reach his hand to his visitor, but could not. But he said very faintly,

"Hello, Father. Just in time."

The priest was moved. He bent down and with his thumb made the sign of the cross on David's forehead, and murmured the first of the prayers for the dying.

It was a hot afternoon in early August, the ninth of August, and the unpainted pine walls, roof and floor of the barracks gave off a resinous heat. There was nobody else in the room but the doctor and Duncan, who had deliberately missed his formation, whatever cost might follow. They asked the chaplain if he preferred that they leave him while he administered the last sacraments. He shook his head, for he knew that when he heard David's confession, his ear would have to be right at David's mouth in order to hear anything at all. He proceeded with the ceremony which made reference to the senses of man, the salt and the water and the oil of the earth, and that bond of spirit between these and man who may perish in the body and return to oil, salt and water, but whose imperishable soul must return to its eternal source.

At his offices, the gaunt chaplain was expert and strong. A certain bitterness showed in his expression, for he was a man too much of the earth, and of the men whom he had loved and served in the war, not to shake his head over the ironical fate of this young officer who must die just as every sign seemed to point to victory and release. Without abdicating his certainty of death as the soul's release to its heaven, the chaplain was yet such a man of sympathy that he could feel what beauties, satisfactions, and hopes must still have remained unrealized in the life that was ending under his blessing. He had been a youth in his time. He knew the tug of the world. In the reality of sacrifice, he could measure what was renounced. He lifted his hand and gave David the Host. David raised his hand a trifle from the bed. The chaplain, smiling broadly as you would smile at a child who tried but could not do what it wanted to do, took the hand and lifted it to David's brow, shoulders and breast, in the sign of the cross.

He was done.

All of this embarrassed the doctor for a little while. He had never seen the sacrament of extreme unction administered before. He was a man of no religion. But he said afterward that when he saw how David responded to the sacrament, he could only wonder.

They were all astonished, even somewhat awed, at the energy that possessed David then for the last hour. Color came into his face, and his mind was lucid at moments. He struggled to sit up, and they eased him by making a pillow of a rolled blanket. He made Duncan sit on the side of the bunk and he took his hand. His eyes were almost flashing with brilliance. The men with him were witness to an extraordinary surge of the last resources of power hidden in that maimed and dying body. The sweat shone on his brow and made his hair curly. It was odd, but Duncan could only think of what he was seeing in these terms: that David was achieving, and was the image of, a superb maturity at this hour, a passionate forecast of the man he would never live to be.

To reach from mind to mind: every day's prosaic human achievement now took on a painful and urgent necessity.

David made them lean close to his head, for he wanted to speak. With unearthly happiness and radiance he said to them that he was ready to die, but first—he waved his hand a little to indicate the barracks, the camp, the enemy; he had to say that though he had been hurt by them, what could he do but forgive them when he believed what he believed at that moment, and felt what he felt now? He said he felt real again for the first time in many months.

Duncan and the doctor exchanged a look.

Forgive their captors? Their cruelty, the idiocy of their vanity, the outrage of their estimate of human life?

Yes, yes, David said to them with his eyes, his scowling smile.

Long afterward, the others could understand what David understood in that imminent moment.

He was saving his powers for a little while, lying back with his eyes shut.

Presently he opened them again and looking as far as he could toward the window, he said to Duncan,

"Deedy, there is a flight of our planes passing overhead. Do you hear them?"

Duncan whispered that yes, yes, he heard them, for if they were going again through David's mind, they were meaningful enough for them all.

That mind could still contain the unlimited sky and a great formation of bombers. To think of its going empty and dark gave Duncan a frantic and helpless feeling. Grinding his hands together he prayed, he willed David to live. The power of light, the unearthly awareness in David at that time, made him feel Duncan's anguish and bitter hope. David looked at him and shook his head. His breath was coming shorter now, and his cheeks were hot and rosy. He motioned Duncan nearer.

He told Duncan to cut it out. This was all right now. This was bigger than anything ever before. He was happy that he could be ready. It was like knowing exactly what you were doing. He touched Duncan's hand. Then he talked of common things. He said he had nothing left to send. His ring had been taken from him long ago. But he wanted to send something else home. He pointed his finger at Duncan, as if to say, You, you must take it for me. He wanted to send them his love, and he wanted them to know that he died without hatred in his heart. "Not hate." He looked, in a sort of sweet absurdity, almost angry as he said it; but it was just his struggle to articulate what crowded his feeling and his thought that made him show strife in his face. He leaned toward Duncan.

"Do you get that, Deedy?"

Duncan said he did. He took David's hand and squeezed it to show that he had the message and would be the one to deliver it.

David lay back with his eyes drowsily opening and shutting. Sweat was on his face. Duncan wiped it off. David was smiling. His beard glistened. The dark hollows under his eyes were glowing with feverish color. At about twenty minutes past four, he rolled his head on the pillow, with a rapid, almost strong gesture, and without opening his eyes but with the same drowsy smile on his lips which shone through his beard, he said,

"Tell them, now," and died.

The chaplain blessed the corpse. They covered it with a blanket.

The doctor and Duncan were exhausted. They felt they had been in communication with the full power of life through the frailest of instruments.

The chaplain closed his little box and rolled it up again in his frayed stole. He said he believed they should all three go right outside now, and dig a grave, and bury the dead.

This is what they did. He put them to work. The heat was still over the island, but the light was lengthening over the mountain. It would not be too long before the mountain would conceal the lowering sun.

When the grave was ready, the three of them carried David's body out to it and laid it in the earth. The chaplain recited prayers in Latin. They then laid David's blanket over him and filled the grave with the turned back earth. It was then that Duncan felt most badly.

Father Zabriski went back to his own camp that evening.

The next day, the doctor and Duncan made a wooden cross and marked the head of David's grave with it. The camp authorities came to look at it expressionlessly, and Duncan was full of what he would do if any one of them so much as touched the cross. But they let it alone, and there it stayed.

A few days later a plane went over and dropped some leaflets, which came twinkling down in the hot sunshine. When the prisoners picked them up and read that the Empire of Japan had surrendered, many of them cried. Curiously, some who were relatively well, now fell ill, as though they no longer must sustain themselves now that rescue was near.

Duncan himself was ill at the time, and did not observe much, but he knew when an American transport plane landed at the airstrip down the island, for he could hear it, and he knew when the American officers it had brought took command of the camp. A week later, a United States Navy cruiser appeared offshore, the prisoners were taken aboard, and the voyage home began.

xlv

When Duncan was at last done, he was shaking. He sat down and lighted a cigarette. The first pull on it made sweat start out on his brow. He felt something akin to guilt. What had he done to her? She was mute and powerless. The pity of the world seemed to be in her face. She gazed at him so ruefully that he saw how she would not really grasp the facts of his story until they might have time—a moment? a day?—to turn into pictures in her mind. He felt curiously free; lightened; but he felt too that he was delivered at her expense. Impulsively, he crossed and bent down to her and took her hands, and with a surge of devotion for the whole course of his relationship to her through David and Eliza, he lifted her hands and kissed them, one after the other. The act astonished him. He had never done anything like it before in his life. He released her and went back and sat down again.

She put her hands to her temples a moment, and then straightened up in her chair.

"I don't know what I can say to thank you," she said. She smiled at him with the very other face of grief. She was ashy pale, there was a sort of archaic grace in her posture, her shoulders drooped, her arms hung like lead, and her body cringed from the savagery and ugliness of the world. But her spirit still strove to preserve itself. Its attempts were what brought his heart up into his mouth.

He knew she was not like other women he knew.

xlvi

Still, he was not prepared for what she said to him presently. For a long interval, she remained silent. He smoked his cigarette through, and tossed the end into the grate. She looked into the coals, then at him, and then out to the last parallels of daylight in the low clouds that hung over the sea. She arose and went to the windows, where she drew the curtains. When she came back and sat down, she said,

"Do you remember that dinner party you gave for us all the year you and David graduated?"

"Yes, certainly. We talked about it at lunch today."

"Yes. And I said I remembered what we—what you and I—talked about that night."

"Yes?"

"Do you remember?"

"Yes."

"I have often thought of it."

"You have, Mrs Hopkinson?"

"I've thought of it all day today. And especially here, this afternoon. Is it still true?"

"Is what still true?"

She shook her head at him, and said,

"I believed you then, that night, and I think it is still true, that you are in love with Liza."

"Oh."

She looked down and then she looked up at him again. It was her famous look. It would always find its goal. Its goal was now the truth.

"Why do you ask?" he asked desperately.

"I am no fool," she said with kindness.

"Well, I cannot answer."

"Why?"

"I have given my word to say nothing."

"You have? To whom. To Liza?"

He ground his teeth and turned away from her and stared into the coals.

"Go and fetch Liza, Duncan. Tell her I would like to see her for just a moment. Bring her yourself. Come with her."

"Oh no. I have promised."

"You have broken no promises. Please."

It was her weariness, showing through all her attempts to conceal it, that moved him. He went.

xlvii

Now that she was alone, the tides swept up within her. She shut her eyes and she heard again what he had told her, and she saw. She was ready to lie down in the darkness and give in to pain. But she told herself that she must not yet do that. The others would be here with her in a moment. She turned her head rapidly from side to side, and blinked against her tears, and made them recede, and made her mind crowd full of what she needed to say. She leaned forward and straightened the painted Mexican box on the table, and then went to the hearth where she took the long handled brush and stroked the ashes back under the iron basket of the grate.

xlviii

When Eliza and Duncan returned they found her tidying the fireplace. She put the brush away and turned. Eliza at a glance saw new in her face the cruel full knowledge which was hers too. She went forward and embraced Dorothy silently. But Dorothy put her off, and asked them to sit down.

"Liza, I think I know something which you know, and which Duncan knows; but it is something I am not supposed to know."

Eliza looked sharply at him, and then back at Dorothy.

"No," said Dorothy, "you are not to blame Duncan, or suspect that he has said anything to me, for he has not. But one evening six years ago, when he gave that dinner party for you and David, in June Week, he sat by me, and he told me that he was very much in love with you then."

Eliza began to blush with misery. She cast her look down, and put her hand to her throat. A variety of protests occurred to her; but when she looked up at Dorothy again, there was no room for denial in an atmosphere so crowded with the truth. She said nothing.

"Well, my darling," continued Dorothy, "you and I have been through some very bad days together, and we have, I think, always been honest. I think we still should be."

Eliza nodded.

"So do I," she said, but her voice was a dry croak. It made Duncan lean forward as if to touch her. But she did not look at him and he subsided.

"I will always love you," said Dorothy, "for thinking first of me. And if nothing else stood in your heart, then I would welcome you, as you know. But Liza, there is something else, and though I must say I had considered it a possibility, I did not believe it seriously until now. But now I know. And so do you. Don't you—don't you, darling?"

There was a burning stubbornness in Eliza. She began to cry.

This overwhelmed Duncan with astonishment. If anybody ought to be crying it was Dorothy. He knelt down next to Eliza and patted not her hand but the cushioned arm of her chair in his attempt to comfort.

"Liza," continued Dorothy, "I can imagine how many times you have turned everything over in your heart. And I can imagine how many times you asked yourself if you would be unfaithful to David and to me if you did what Duncan wants you to do. Haven't you?"

Eliza bent lower and covered her face with her hands.

"Well, my darling, I do not think of it that way. Do you know what I think? I think it is better to make life than to remember it."

At this, Eliza came from her chair and went to Dorothy and buried her face in her neck and wept like a child. Dorothy put her arms around the girl and murmured into her hair, and stroked her head, and presently set her away a little distance so they could look into each other's eyes.

"I am right, Eliza, am I not?"

Eliza said, in a crowded voice,

"Yes, Doro. But I meant you never to know."

"I know that."

Duncan was becalmed by the stormy scene.

Dorothy stood up.

"I do not want to arrange a thing for you both, or about either of you. But I do want you to know that as far as I am concerned, you are wholly free, and if you plan to be married, you have my blessings and my love." She paused. "And I believe you would have David's, too."

The young people took each other's hand. Duncan kissed Eliza, formally and politely.

"Oh, Doro, I can never—how did you know? I made him promise on his honor to say nothing."

"When?"

"This afternoon, out driving."

Dorothy smiled.

"Well, Duncan told me nothing except by his silence. But last evening, his heart was full and hopeful, and he spoke to Wick. Wick told Diana. Diana told me. I am very glad she did. It was something only a very close friend could manage, I think. Now darling, you should powder your nose and go back downstairs. I am not coming."

She then took Duncan's hand and pressed it, kissed Eliza on the cheek, and let them out her door. She went into her bedroom where there was no light but the glow from the rooms downstairs on the bare trees outside. She lay down on her bed alone with images.

She was so appalled with pity that she could only lie there and gaze into the darkness of her ceiling. She felt ugly within and without, and ashamed, as if she had blundered into knowledge to which she had no right; or into danger of a sort which gave her fear for her body, and from which she must recoil in silence because she was too terrified to scream, as if walking she had found herself beset by creatures of mindless menace.

xlix

A while later there was a cheerful knock at the door of her sitting room. In the darkness she arose and touched her drawn cheeks. She caught her breath. Actually, she did not want to answer the door, but her habit was stronger than her desire. As she crossed the dark bedroom and came into the sitting room she unconsciously assumed an expression of interest and grace with which to open the door. She did not know who knocked. But whoever it was, she thought, he had no right to her grief. When she opened the door, she amended her thought, for there was perhaps the only one to whom she would show it unconditionally. It was Avy.

He gave her a little bow from the hips, and said that he was needing a breath of air after the party. Everybody had gone. He thought her very sensible to have drifted away quietly for forty winks. But now perhaps she would put on a coat and take a little turn with him? He wanted to walk down to the water and back. How about it?

She put out her hand and touched him on the forearm, silently thanking him for coming. She went to the other room and took up a coat, and came back. They marched downstairs to the ground floor without seeing anybody. Avy found his cap and topcoat, and they let themselves out into the hedged court of the driveway. He tucked his arm through hers and set a lazy strolling pace. It was a warm evening, for January. The moon had risen. There was a hint of its pallor on the river. They said nothing.

In her arm he could feel the deep weariness of her whole self. He marvelled privately at Vivi's intuitions. She had told him to go up and see about Dorothy.

They came to the water's edge. There was a playful minia-ture peacefulness about the wavelets that passed endlessly up the Severn, and lapped at the dock and the boathouse and the embankment where they stood.

He felt her about to speak. He hoped he might have something to say to help her. But she said,

"It was a very nice party, wasn't it, Avy? I saw so many people I hadn't seen for years."

"That's nice. They all loved seeing you."

"Do you have people in every Sunday afternoon?"

"Yes. Even when I'm away, Vivi has them in. Once her duty is plain. Hell and highwater and so on."

She was trying to go back with him to everyday attitudes. For the first time in all their lives he felt constrained in her presence. He took her hand.

"Doro!"

"I know, Avy. I cannot help it, but oh, the way it was!"

"I am not sure he should have told you any of it at all."

"Oh yes. I am. I would not have let him withhold anything. I am sure he knew that. I am sure from the way he kept looking at me, and the way I kept looking at him."

The evening was not cold. A shred of mist was gathering between them and the moon. It was not the weather that made her begin to shake. He tightened his hug of her arm, and said to himself that he was glad he could be with her at the moment. He said softly, with a grain of fond humor in his voice that recalled so much to them both,

"Well, Doro?"

She turned her head to his shoulder and cried with all the honor of a broken heart. He had never in all their years of close alliance and common sorrow seen her lose her composure. He smiled over her head when he thought that she would be grateful for the darkness of evening and the clouding of the moon, so that even he might not clearly see her woe. He held her closely about her shoulders, and patted her quietly. She tried to control herself; but her gasping sobs were some moments in dying down. Ruefully she said,

"I was filled with such ugly rage and sorrow."

"Yes, yes, my dearie."

"It was so odd, all the while he was talking, I kept seeing many things, the things he was describing, and at the same time, all the things long ago, when David was little."

She could not go on. She began to cry again. She shook her head, humble before her own weakness.

He knew how she loved the little amenities and comforts of everyone to continue, no matter what; so with his free hand he took a cigarette and his lighter and began to smoke. It was just the small offhand reference to the simple world which could restore her.

She looked up again presently, and went on.

"I nearly died when I remembered as I was listening, how David was in his little swimming suit at Honolulu that year when we were all there together. We had a snapshot of him that day. I still have it, with his feet in the water and his head bent, and the sunlight making a crown of light on his bleached hair. He had a tin shovel in one hand and in the other a broken sea shell, one of those cowries, I suppose. He was dreaming with some plan. I don't know what."

Silence, while her last words echoed in their minds. Who would ever know?

Winking against the tears that suffused her eyes, she said,

"His body was brown, and so perfect, that little boy of five, isn't that the most wonderful and commonplace discovery?

Every mother makes it, seeing her child created so beautifully. So beautifully."

She fell silent again. Finally she added,

"One thing, Avy. Duncan made me see how extraordinary it was when David died, for he swears it was the most unearthly kind of knowledge he ever saw. Something happened to him at the very last. As if he were suddenly able to understand everything and forgive everything. It is that which I must remember. It was that that he wanted me to know."

"Does it help you?" asked Avy, looking grimly at the playing water.

"It must, it must, Avy. After what I have heard, I don't think I could live if I didn't forgive just as he did. There would be no way to bear it. That is what he left for me to know."

"Yes. Yes. Well, there are many things I shall never understand, for I do not have certain kinds of cleverness, but one thing I have never had any doubt about is the potential inside dimension of a man. I think we'll all understand that more and more about David, as time goes on. —As it does of course."

She freed herself from his arm and kissed his cheek.

"Dear Avy."

They turned to walk back up the quiet street.

"Well, Avy," she said presently, "speaking of time going on. I must tell you about Liza and Duncan. See if you think I did right."

He listened, and then said he believed that she had done right. He would be interested to see if Vivi thought so, too.

At the house, they found her writing notes at her tall desk, for there were still a few minutes before she was going to give them all a buffet supper. The house was quiet and she enjoyed her correspondence. As she finished each note, she folded it, sealed it in its envelope, stamped it, and sailed it to the floor. In a matter of a very few minutes she could have her rug littered. It was a fooling sort of disorder, which she enjoyed sweeping away when it was time to gather all the envelopes to be mailed.

She turned and saw at once that her sister had been through something. But she saw too, and she looked devotedly at Avy about it, that she had come a long way back to herself. What she didn't understand was the waggish air about Avy. She said,

"Avy, what are you trying so desperately to have me ask you about?"

Dorothy burst out into a little laugh, it was like the utmost peace, this family humor, and she went over to Vivi and bent down and looked into her eyes and then kissed her on the forehead.

"A piece of news," said Avy, "I leave it to Doro."

Vivi shifted her much enlivened eyes toward her sister. Dorothy replied,

"I told Avy what I had done this afternoon, in talking to Duncan and Liza."

"Why *Liza?*"

"They are going to be married."

"But Liza is to be with you!"

"No. I told them they must go ahead."

Vivi had the ability to project her thoughts and opinions plainly. They watched her, and could almost rehearse with her, thought by thought, in a rather majestic train of logic and order, the implications of this information. She did not say anything at all until she had completed her whole pattern of

214

attitudes toward the idea. Then she looked at her sister, and with a certain severity to modify sentiment, and conscious of their whole past, she said,

"Dorothy, I think you are the most wonderful person in the world."

1

Later in the evening, Eliza and Duncan appeared. The Graces congratulated them, and Vivi said, with a hint of anxious perplexity,

"Eliza, I do hope you believe I was acting for what I thought best all around?"

"Oh, I do, I do, Aunt Vivi."

"No," said Vivi, "you see, I could think of nothing else but my dear sister's immediate future. You must have thought me blind to yours. But how could I have known? I wish you and Duncan the dearest happiness."

"Thank you, Aunt Vivi, for both of us. —We do plan a fairly long engagement. We both feel we want to become ourselves, again, first, if you know what I mean."

Duncan scowled, for he thought Vivi too visibly relieved to hear that a suitable interval would be allowed to pass before the marriage should occur.

"But of course," continued Eliza, "we want you all to be present, and Aunt Vivi, I know you will understand if I say I especially want Doro."

This was referred to Dorothy by Vivi, with a glance.

Dorothy waited a second before replying, and they were not sure, but it was possible that she had a start of tears in her eyes, but it came to nothing, and she said,

"Liza, my darling, I do not think I will come. There are some things that ought to start completely fresh. I know I am right. And what is more, there is a limit to what I think I can trust myself to endure. I would be remembering, my dear, while you would be looking ahead. It is right for you; but not for me. I love you both very much. But I cannot attend."

li

After several weeks of rest and comfort with her sister and Avy, Dorothy went back to California. On the way, she stopped off in New Mexico for a few days, at the urgent request of Jack and Eleanor Abbott. The idea suited her. They had much to talk about. She had old friends to see, and deep draughts of landscape and sky to take. But actually, these were not the reasons why she had come. One afternoon she asked Mrs Abbott to drive her out to the cemetery of Crystal Wells. Dorothy had not been there since the last year of Little Farm. Mrs Abbott stayed in the car. Dorothy walked over to her husband's grave. She was alone. She came here to prove this, to risk weakness, and to survive it.

AFTER THE STORY

The characters in this novel are fictional composites of many individuals encountered in the events, relationships, and atmospheres, of the period. There is no intention to depict biographically any actual persons associated with the United States Navy.

59